In the Shadow of the Dead
A Journal of the Final Plague
By Alan McBride
With photos by Alan McBride

IN THE SHADOW OF THE DEAD

First edition. October 8, 2024.

Copyright © 2024 Alan McBride.

ISBN: 979-8227442437

Written by Alan McBride.

Notes and Copyright

This is a work of fiction. As stated earlier, all of the characters, events, and organizations portrayed in this book are either used fictitiously or are a product of the author's imagination. Any resemblance to real events and/or to real persons living or dead is unintended and completely coincidental.

The photographs in this work represent the work of the author. Where people are identifiable, written permission to use the images has been obtained from the subjects. In situations where photos were taken at public events, subjects were made aware at the time that their images would appear in published media. However, these images have been edited to ensure the subjects remain unidentifiable.

The publishers and author do not consent to any Artificial Intelligence (AI), Generative AI, large language model, machine learning chatbot, or other automated analysis, generative process, or replication program to reproduce, mimic, remix, summarize, or otherwise replicate any part of this novel, via any means: print, graphic, sculpture, multimedia, audio, or any other medium in existence or to be invented. We support the right of humans to control their artistic works.

Cover design by Getcovers.

Dedications

This book is dedicated to everybody who strives to create, regardless
of the medium.
Never give up.
And to Tux.
Miss you, buddy.

Introduction

When I began writing this book, I had no idea I was writing a book.

Let me explain.

A few years ago, I thought it would be fun to write a 'diary' about the onset of a mysterious virus and the total collapse of civilization, and publish it on a popular social media site. It seemed like a fun thing to do to keep people entertained. The diary never gained a large following, but that was fine with me. It was just meant to entertain a few of us as we followed in the footsteps of this traveler.

Well, time got away from me and other responsibilities piled up, and I gave serious thought to deleting the diary and calling it a day. That's when the unexpected hit me. I realized that I had not been keeping a diary. I had been starting to tell a story, and I knew how it would end. What you are reading is that diary, updated and fleshed out. It has been a fascinating journey, and it isn't over. In telling *this* story I found other stories waiting to be told, all of them populated by some remarkable people. I'm working on those stories now. In the meantime, I hope you enjoy this introduction to a boundless world where there is so much more than meets the eye.

I've set rules for the virus in this tale and I've worked to stick by them. That's important if a story is to have internal consistency. In terms of geography, you'll find that things don't always line up with what many of us know. I assure you the reasons for that will become clear; but in the meantime, no spoilers.

I was starting to put this together as a novel when Covid came on the scene, and that pandemic forced me to take a hard look at my early drafts and reevaluate them. Given everything that was going on during that time, it became clear to me that parts of the story weren't going to hold up. I made some necessary changes, and the result is a story that gives you permission to believe this could happen.

The original diary, by the way, is still out there. It's archived and about all that remains is the title, but if you google 'Dispatches from the Zombie War,' you'll find it. Feel free to check in.

Cheers!

Alan McBride

Autumn 2024

Prologue

When we try to remember things, we look through the lens of flawed recollection and hindsight. On occasion, we do remember past mistakes and learn from them. It's in that rare spirit that I write these words. Here is a record of my travels, my encounters, my mistakes, and the world in which they took place. Conversations, when they appear, have been written as soon after the events as possible. In some cases, I have needed to draw on my memory. When that has been the case, I have worked diligently to be faithful to this journal. It's my hope, if any people are left to read these words, that they may learn from them.

I write this chronicle as if I were a man standing graveside, reflecting on a life that expended a last fitful breath before growing still and silent. The grave, though, is that of a civilization that once spanned a planet and reached for the heavens. And there is no rest here, no peaceful silence. The grave by which I stand is empty, for the dead have climbed out of it and tread across a world that should tremble at their weight.

The civilization I once knew, the world on which we all once depended, may now be gone past all reckoning. An entire world may be nothing more than ashes, brought low by an illness that swept away all before it with a complete disregard for station and boundaries.

The disease came on the winds of a crisp October and seemed to spread as if by flash fire. By the end of the month, lit by flickering street lamps, civilization seemed to falter, to hold its breath. We found ourselves balanced on a razor's edge. On either side lay the topple ... and the long fall into darkness. I do not know how this will end, or if it has ended already.

To this day, I don't know how the plague of the undead began, except that the agent was a virus. Where did it first take root? How did it manage to spread with such a ferocity? I leave those questions for others, for those who know more than I.

My name is Jake, and here is where I leave my own stories of the plague's early days, and the days that came after.

May there be a future that will remember us.

Day One

We should have noticed this earlier. But I guess every road leading to disaster has signs along the way of "pay attention, this is important" or "last chance to turn things around" and they all get ignored equally. In our defense, at least locally, we were all focused on making the most out of the last of summer. Besides, this is Miami, and unless the news is about an approaching hurricane, it has to be really big to get our attention.

Word of a new disease came in early September, but the cases were rare and isolated and, like I said, nobody was paying much attention. Hell, I shrugged it off, thinking it was just another early visit from the flu. When cases started accelerating in the last part of the month, it was still ignored. People dismissed it with words like "overreaction," "hoax," and the ever popular, "Big Pharma just wants to make money off of nothing."

Yeah, "nothing" indeed. I doubt that. I started getting edgy about this bug shortly after the news began getting through the usual background noise of cold and flu season, so here in late September, I've decided to keep a journal. I figure if I put all my worries on the page where I can see them, I'll be able to whittle them down to their proper size.

Maybe, a year or so from now, I'll be able to look at these pages and have a good laugh at myself.

Day Two

Well, reading the headlines was a mistake. I'm getting the sense that nobody quite knows what this disease is, but medical people are getting increasingly nervous about it. The news is heavy on worry but short on details. According to the media, the medical establishment suspects this is a virus, but there's not much more coming out than that. I've been hearing that cases are accelerating; that we're headed toward an epidemic.

And I've been hearing darker stuff, too, such as half-whispered stories about what is happening to the people who are infected. It's not much more than rumor, and I hope that's all it turns out to be, but it's costing me sleep already. My edgy, nervous feelings haven't gone away. They may be getting worse.

Oh, well. Tomorrow is October first, and I think I need to get out of the house and out of my own head, maybe do a little shopping.

Halloween always cheers me up.

Day Three

The news broke today that this disease, whatever it is, has an insanely high mortality rate. Nobody is saying how high, but nobody is reporting any recoveries. That's not the worst of it, either. The reports say that nobody is taking time for burials. The dead go straight from the morgue to the nearest crematorium.

Official channels have not confirmed this, but the media that broke the news are standing by their anonymous sources and aren't backing off a word of it.

So, what we have is a vacuum of information, and it's being filled with some of the most insane conspiracy noise I have ever heard. Talk radio, and the less reliable media, are saying this is a government conspiracy meant to hide a new bioweapon being tested on civilians, or they're shouting that it's all a hoax meant to stoke the cold flames of fear and deliver us to martial law.

One episode really stands out, though, and it chills me every time I think about it. A caller to a local talk show said things were more frightening than we could imagine. The caller identified herself as a trauma nurse at a local hospital, and she spoke with the kind of silent, desperate urgency that can make you stop still and listen. She started describing what she was seeing but the talk show host, a guy who swears this is all a hoax, wasn't having any of it. He began yelling and railing at the nurse, shouting her down almost immediately. He didn't let her finish the call, either. He pulled the plug on her fast.

But I remember her last whisper before the host cut the call: "They don't stay dead."

Day Four

More Halloween shopping for me today — leaving work and heading straight to my favorite stores. The season is taking my mind off developing events at least a little, but I'd be a liar if I said it cleared my mind completely. The unease that I started feeling a few days ago has become a constant thing, as persistent as a shadow.

Everybody at the stores has been pleasant. Clerks, customers, it doesn't matter. People are going out of their way to be cheerful and welcoming. All of us have become social animals and chatterboxes, glad to see another person. I've seen more smiles and manners in the last few days than I've seen in months.

The cheerfulness, however, feels forced. With every greeting and conversation there is a restless undercurrent of unease. Behind every smile there are eyes darting nervously, looking for anything that could be out of place or a little bit wrong. You can also see it in the pattern of shopping. Anything related to vampires, witches, werewolves, all that sort... it's being scooped up. The zombies, on the other hand, are being left alone. Nobody is touching that merchandise.

We're doing our best to be cheerful, but every day it feels more like we're whistling past the graveyard.

Day Five

Something unsettling is going on here.

On my drive to work, I noticed more uniformed police on the roads. I hadn't heard of any holiday speed enforcement efforts or seatbelt checks, so this all struck me as unusual. There were too many cops for a normal workday.

Then there were the traffic stops. I only saw a couple, but the cops moved fast, and they always, always had back-up. As soon as the car stopped, the cops stepped out with guns drawn and leveled. Megaphones instructed drivers to step out of the car with their hands in the air.

I saw frightened drivers facing nervous cops on a hair trigger, and I would swear that the cops were more frightened than the drivers. It's as though they were on the look-out for something beyond the ordinary and they were absolutely terrified of finding it.

This afternoon, leaving work, I saw more police activity. Two cruisers full of cops stopped near a homeless-looking guy staggering along the side of the road. I heard them yell for him to stop and raise his hands. He didn't do any of that. He just turned and started staggering toward the officers.

The cops immediately opened fire on him. I swear they must have emptied their guns, but this guy kept moving, staggering toward them without any notice of the bullets pounding into him. It took a headshot to bring him down. And he was moaning a low, unearthly sound right up to the last.

The really scary part? He didn't bleed at all. The bullets thumped into his chest and left marks on his shirt, but that was all. No bleeding, only a nerve-scraping moan, and a drive to stagger toward the police who were doing their best to stop him cold.

No living thing could have survived all of that.

Day Six

More proof that things are going sideways, as if any more proof is needed.

I had been in the parking lot of a strip center, picking up a few necessary groceries, when I saw an altercation blow up completely. I'm glad it all happened after I got my groceries and was packing them in the car. Otherwise, I'm not sure how I'd have handled things. As it was, I had the shakes all the way home.

I was packing my groceries when I heard somebody raising their voice and making some kind of scene. I turned and saw a woman yelling and shaking her fist at some guy. The target of her temper was shambling around with a glazed look, and everyone else was walking well clear of him and keeping quiet. Not this woman. She was standing right in the path of the guy, screeching at him at the top of her voice. She was yelling about how this was all a hoax and how he was an actor on somebody's payroll. She kept on screaming about how she could see through this "performance," and she wasn't going to let him get away with this and she was going to prove it to everybody.

By this time, somebody had called the cops and a couple of police cruisers pulled up. When the officers got out, the woman demanded that the cops arrest the "actor" and shame him into being a "normal person." Instead of doing what the woman demanded, one of the officers calmly asked her to step back from the shambling man and let them handle things. I have got to give that officer credit. He was cool and never raised his voice. He kept asking the woman to walk over to the cruisers and let them deal with the situation.

That really set her off. If the police were calm, she was anything but that. She snapped a profanity-laden load of vitriol at the officers and marched toward the shambler, cursing about how she was going to show the cops "how to do their goddam jobs."

Maybe she heard the low moaning that was starting to come from the guy, or maybe not. All I know is, noise or no noise, it didn't stop her from winding her arm back to deliver a powerful slap.

The slap never landed. The thing struck like a snake, sinking its teeth into the woman's hand right at the wrist. She screamed, a real scream this time, and tried to pull her hand out of the thing's mouth. It hung on while she panicked and tugged as hard as she could. I heard tearing, like fabric, and saw her pulling back her hand. God, but it was a mess. I could see bones showing through what was left of it. It looked less like a hand and more like a tangle of raw meat.

The shambler began closing in on the woman even as she tried to stagger back from it. Maybe it was drawn by her screaming, or maybe by the smell of blood. Maybe it was something else altogether. I was just glad to see the cops stepping forward, weapons drawn.

I could see, then, why the police hadn't acted earlier to stop the shambler. They had been waiting for a clear shot, and they couldn't get one. The woman had been in their way. Now that she had staggered clear of the shambler, the officers aimed and fired. Two shots, both in the head. The guy dropped instantly.

What I saw next will probably haunt me for a very long time. One of the cops turned toward the woman, who was still screaming and clutching the ruins of her hand. He spoke to her with the same calm voice he'd used when he tried to get her to move out of the way.

"I'm sorry, ma'am, but we tried to get you to move. We only wanted to get you to safety. I'm really sorry... I just wanted you to know that."

He aimed his pistol and fired. One shot to her head. She fell and twitched a moment, then went still.

I lost my lunch.

It's a miracle that I made it home after witnessing that.

It's now four in the morning. I haven't slept. I can't sleep.

Day Seven

The news is out, and it is not good.

All major networks broke into their programming for a special report from the White House today. It's never a good sign when every network drops what it's doing and informs viewers that something big is coming and they really need to tune in for this. Even the streaming networks halted their live programming.

Sure enough, at the appointed time, both the President and Vice President were on every screen, with faces looking as grim as death. But they didn't really say anything beyond a few introductory words. The bulk of the news conference was taken up by medical professionals.

Just a couple of minutes into the news conference, and I could understand why every face on the screen was devastatingly sober. The medical professionals, epidemiologists, confirmed that a novel virus was loose, and they were still trying to understand and dissect it.

The virus had been identified by a couple of doctors at the World Health Organization, Asher Argus and Maxine Jones, and they already knew a couple of things about it. First, the virus didn't appear to be easily communicable. It looked like the only way to catch it was to be bitten by one of the infected. That was the good news.

The bad news was that the virus was one hundred percent contagious. If you were bitten, you were infected. Simple as that. The doctors said, based on what they knew, that the incubation period was between twelve and thirty-six hours. If you were bitten, you had that much time before full infection set in.

By "full infection," I got the impression they meant "clinical death and reanimation."

You see, these doctors were doing their best to spin this with statements about how they were working on an early treatment, or even a vaccine, and that there was plenty of reason to hope but, yes, it did appear that after the initial contact a person would become increasingly ill until a day or so had passed and all vital signs had stopped.

And then had restarted.

The doctors were very circumspect in their language, but eventually it became clear that, a few moments after clinical death, something came back. Nobody was saying what exactly was happening here, whether the "appearance of death" was part of the disease pathology or if it was something else.

And what could it be, this "something else?"

Yeah. That's the big question, the one with no real answer just yet.

Everybody was being "cautiously optimistic" about a treatment and an eventual vaccine, but everybody was being pretty evasive, too.

And, yes, they could confirm reports that some bodies had gone missing from some morgues, and they would inform us when they had more information to pass along.

When the news conference ended, some of the networks provided a summary. Everything was disturbingly clear and aimed at preserving calm. For once, nobody tried to sensationalize anything. For once, there may have been no way to sensationalize what we all had just heard.

And we all pretended that nobody was thinking of the words "undead" and "zombie."

Day Eight

Right now, there's the sense that people are still trying to make things work... but that hope was losing a little more ground from one day to the next.

The talking heads are still all over television, radio, and the web. Everyone has been talking about how it's "still early in the game" and how people are working on treatments or even a cure, but nobody sounds as confident as they did less than a week ago.

We still don't know what happened with the re-animates that have escaped from the morgues, or if they have managed to infect others. But I get an uneasy sense of change for the worse.

On the streets, sometimes you'll hear a low moan... or see a figure moving with that slow, disconnected stride that seems to be something that belongs to these re-animates.

God. I've not once used the word "people" to describe them. I guess "zombie" is what works.

Re-animate... damn, but that's too clinical by half.

It's all changing out there. It feels like it's starting to shake apart.

Day Nine

They've begun setting up quarantine zones in various places, acting like this is still something that can be contained. Personally, I'm not so sure. The disease, despite everybody's assurances to the contrary, seems to be gaining ground on us. I ask myself, if things are as secure as everybody swears they are, then why are we setting up these quarantine zones? And why are they getting bigger? And why do people never seem to leave them?

Case in point: I snapped a quick photo of a young person in one of the quarantine zones; this one set up at a local high school. The person turned, went from living to something else, even as my shutter clicked. It's strange, but you can see the light and the intelligence behind those eyes right up till the end. Then, you see a shudder and hear a death-rattle.

Then the people look up again ... and those eyes appear dull and filmed over, opaque. But they see you. Even as slate gray, they bore into you.

They say the eyes are the windows to the soul. And, God, there's the nightmare. What kind of soul stares from behind the blank walls of those eyes? I don't know, but I get the shivers every time I think about it.

Day Ten

Meet   the   enemy.

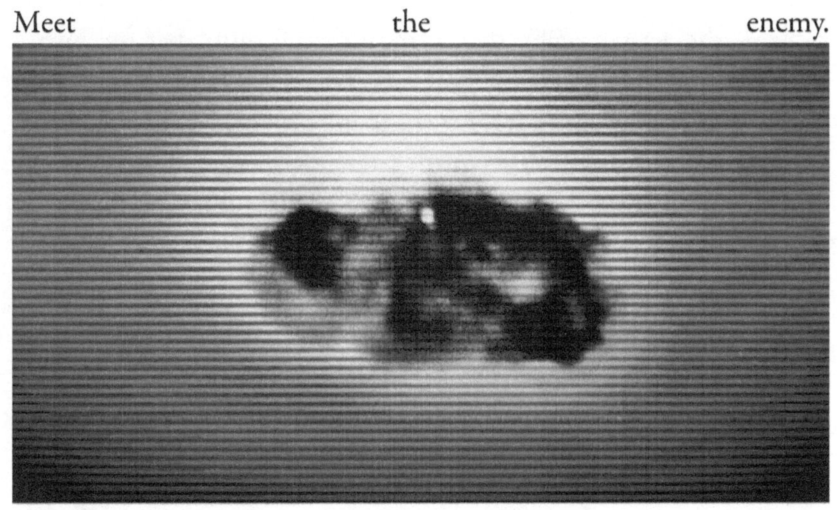

The news broadcasted this image today— an electron micrograph of what they are calling the Argus/Jones virus, named after the epidemiologists who first isolated it. This ordinary-looking blob is the lethal agent that can turn a healthy person into a shambling husk driven by the sole imperative of self-propagation.

Scientists now admit it turns the living into the reanimated dead.

Argus/Jones, invisible to the naked eye, converts a human of any size into an instinct-driven robot fashioned of decaying flesh.

Based on what the scientific community has been able to figure out, this virus appears to function by shutting down most major organ systems and re-wiring the brain; some elements of the mind are physically changed, others are wiped entirely. We don't yet know to what degree this takes place, since "kill-shots" have to destroy the brain case.

We do know that Argus/Jones is probably natural and got in under our radar. And how did that happen, you may wonder? Well, it may be that we just got too good at keeping secrets, all of us.

The health officials in the nation of origin for Argus/Jones kept things quiet for reasons they alone know. International stigma? External fears? Internal bureaucracy? I doubt that it matters, not anymore.

We know that, in the US, Argus/Jones was first detected by one of our homeland intelligence agencies. The agency officials were concerned that it might represent a test of a weaponized bio-agent, so they instructed their analysts and medical people to study the virus but tell no one about it.

Not even the Centers for Disease Control.

The official word was silence, until hospitals started reporting cases, and CDC officials began testing on their own.

We have no idea how many people were infected by the time the CDC had begun to figure this out and the intelligence administrators chose to break their agency's official silence. Even then, as late as September, we might have turned the tide.

But we had become too good at something else: denial.

Too many people refused to accept the growing amount of evidence. Too many people were too willing to ignore what they were seeing with their own eyes, day after day, and too many people were willing to hold that line while infections snowballed, and the rate of propagation grew to something never witnessed in our history.

Would an earlier alert have helped us fight this better? Would some word from somebody, anybody, have bought us more time or given us more of a chance at a sober understanding of what we were all facing? I don't know.

All I know is we became too good at keeping secrets; too good at looking the other way.

And that may take us to our graves.

Day Eleven

Things took a turn for the worse today, and I'm beginning to think this is a battle we may not win.

Scientists confirmed today that Argus/Jones had spread more than initially suspected, and that we may be dealing with far more re-animates than everybody first believed. Seems that lots of people, once infected, are choosing to keep it a secret. On the one hand, I can see their point. Nobody wants to go into a quarantine zone knowing they won't be coming out again. On the other hand, we all know how this disease ends, so why would a person choose to risk infecting their family ... knowing what would happen to them?

I suppose one of the things that drives the secrecy is the same thing that drives people to get lottery tickets. Sure, the odds of getting lucky are stacked astronomically against you. But what if you may be the lucky person? Why not take the chance? What is there to lose?

What could possibly go wrong?

Day Twelve

I've started getting supplies together just in case things go to hell after all.

The list of purchases looks like I'm planning to camp out in the middle of a war zone— starter's pistol and ammunition, hunting bow and arrows, tent, water purification tablets, all you need for an extended stay in the great outdoors ... provided the outdoors are something out of a post-apocalyptic movie.

It took more thought and planning than I'd expected. There are so many ideas that look sensible at first but are worthless when you reconsider them.

Take batteries, for instance. If the power is down for an extended period, how many extra batteries should I have for the things that need them? Better just to get a hand-charger and maybe one extra set of batteries. Problem solved.

I've been trying to keep the purchases light, sensible, and smart. But it's still a learning curve with all that. Lesson One came today, when a front rolled in and dropped a ton of rain. When it stops, I'm going out to get a poncho and some waterproofing for my boots and outerwear.

Note to self: get a bicycle. And make sure the most vital stuff can be put in a backpack or hung on a belt. Best to be ready if things take a nosedive and gasoline becomes something impossible to get.

So far, my purchases have set me back about three alimony payments, but I'm not all that worried about it. One of the advantages of an amiable divorce. My ex-wife and I are still on good terms, so she'll understand if the payments are late. She knows I've always been good for the money. I should call her and make sure she's doing okay.

Maybe I'm being paranoid ... I really hope so.

But I get this feeling that being able to carry what I need will mean the difference between dead and alive.

It feels like I'm going to find out soon.

Day Thirteen

I heard them outside my home tonight.

There was the shuffling of feet, anarchic motion of barely coordinated bodies ... low moans that were somewhere between a sob and a howl, low and drawn out.

I kept as quiet as I could ... silent as the grave, they say ... and looked out. Saw the dim figures shuffling past. Took a quick picture. God, I was quiet, so quiet, but the click of the shutter sounded like a rifle shot.

The government says everything is under control; that the outbreak is being contained.

This picture says we're being lied to.

Day Fourteen

Another night where sleep has been a thing hoped for, but not achieved. The racket of gunfire is a staccato soundtrack to the flickering orange of downtown on fire.

High-pitched wailing of sirens and low moaning of the restless dead blended in what I would swear is a dirge.

Sometimes it feels like the undead sense what has been lost to them, when night is in its blackest deep.

The moaning raises hackles and drags fingertips across a blackboard then.

I miss the nights when traffic and police sirens counted for silence...

Day Fifteen

I just got word that the Seven Mile Bridge, linking the Florida mainland to the Florida Keys, has been fortified. The bridge is part of that long ribbon of US Highway 1, and it's a critical connection. Without it, the only traffic between the mainland and the Lower Keys is either by boat or by vigorous swimming. Fortifications are unheard of, so I consider this a sign that people in the Keys are getting very nervous about the current state of things.

The authorities have set up checkpoints, and people are being screened for signs of early infection. A friend of mine says the bridge has been mined, and they're preparing to sever the connection if the Miami outbreak gets out of hand.

I'm worried about what could happen if that idea backfires. Imagine being trapped on an island chain, with a growing army of re-animates at your back, and with no way out.

Day Sixteen

Work took me to Marathon today. The area is near the South Florida terminus of the Seven Mile Bridge. While I was there I took a good long look. At my back were the Upper Keys and the Florida mainland. In front of me, almost lost in the distance, were the Middle and Lower Keys. Everything was connected by that long and durable span of steel and concrete which still managed to look pretty damn fragile.

There it was, the only way to drive to the mainland, and I've got a feeling my memory is going to last a lot longer than the bridge.

That's how things look after today.

I was near the bridge this afternoon when I saw one of the guards almost nose-to-nose with somebody trying to get across on a bicycle.

I couldn't tell exactly what was going on, since both men were yelling in Spanish, and I don't speak a word of it. But it was heated, I could tell that.

The guy with the bicycle decided to push his way through the checkpoint, yelling and shaking his fist at everybody.

Then, cool as you please, the guard pulled his gun and put a single round into the other man.

He wasn't thrown back by the shot or anything like what you see in the movies. No, he just stood there for a minute, looking stupidly at the hole in his chest ... like he couldn't quite figure it out. Then he crumpled to the pavement and twitched a couple of times before going still.

The people manning the checkpoint rolled the limp body of the man off the bridge and into the channel. They pitched his bike in after him.

Everybody on that bridge was so quiet. You could hear the splashes from the body and bike clearly. They echoed through the afternoon.

So much silence in those moments. But packed with so much tension.

Things are on the edge of losing control.

It's all hanging by a string. And a blade is cutting its way through

...

Day Seventeen

The Florida Keys have severed their connection to the mainland.

Late last night, the people manning the checkpoint fell back toward Little Duck Key, ignited the charges on the Seven Mile Bridge, and blew the entire span into the sky. You could hear the blast echo toward south Florida.

I'm not surprised, really, not after what happened yesterday. After the confrontation on the bridge, and the shooting, it would have been a miracle if we'd managed to cool things down at all. As it was, things just kept getting more tense, more anxious, and angrier as yesterday went along.

So... BOOM ... and that settles that.

My friend in Key West says this had been coming, and all the tourists and visitors were given the opportunity to leave. Nobody wanted to go.

I hope it works out for them.

Here, I'm not so sure.

Florida has declared a state of emergency for Miami-Dade, Monroe, Broward, and Palm Beach County and has called in the National Guard. It looks like all the state will follow, and soon.

The governor called a news conference and admitted that nothing was off the table. He said if things don't get contained in the next day or two, the state could take "more drastic steps."

More drastic steps. Not sure I like the sound of that.

It makes me feel like somebody is walking on my grave.

Day Eighteen

I've been checking the house, making sure that there aren't any weak points ... places that will help them get inside. The occasional low moan ... sometimes followed by the crack of a firearm ... gives me a lot of motivation there, I can tell you.

A home that's kept out the burglars for years suddenly feels flimsy and vulnerable.

The cops are keeping it professional, with a growing presence on the streets and anywhere you can put a uniform, but I can tell the strain is getting to them.

It's all done wonders for the city crime rate, though. Guess that tells us how bad it has to get before most of the vandals take the day off. On the other hand, maybe a lot of them found the streets a little too mean and learned it a little too late.

Imagine being the mugger or rapist who accidentally picks a re-animate for a target. That's active street justice right there.

Empty parking spaces at work today. Not too many, but enough to notice.

I wonder how the place will look by the end of the month, or if I'll be here to notice.

Day Nineteen

The horrific and the heroic were on display in my city last night, and I had a front-row seat.

It began when I saw riot police walking past the burning hulk of a car. The thing went up in a geyser of hot metal and gasoline vapor, and they didn't even flinch.

An explosion and fire near a gas storage facility lit the night with a burst of blood-orange sunlight before fading to the steady glow of an unchecked fire. Within minutes, sirens informed us that the fire crews were on the way.

It's times like these that highlight a superhuman level of dedication among the firefighters, the street cops, and the National Guard. I saw them all fighting the fires and the re-animates lured by the sounds of shouts and burning structures. Everybody just dug in. They knew the odds were impossible, but they fought for every inch of ground.

The firefighters and everybody supporting them were ordered to fall back. I heard the orders crackling from every two-way radio. I heard everyone, and I mean everyone, getting the order to retreat. And I saw everyone glance at their radios, shrug, and get back to business.

Not sure how much heart there was in those orders, to be honest. It's a hateful thing to abandon your city, to abandon your home, to fire and the undead.

To their credit, the firefighters did get most of the fires under control. They let some of the other blazes keep burning, but it looked like those weren't going to spread anyway. A measure of good news for all of us at a time when good news is in dangerously short supply.

The cops and the guard were methodical to the point of being machines. No crazy suppressing fire was laid down here, just the cool squeeze of one single shot after another, taking down the re-animates one by one. Shots, flat and evenly spaced, then the pause to reload, then the shots again. Steady as the ticking of a metronome.

Nobody quit. Nobody fell back until hammers fell on empty guns. Even then, the firefighters made sure they had packed all their gear before they moved out. The cops and the guard stayed with them. When they finally left the area, I left with them. Nobody seemed to mind this civilian starting his car and leaving the scene, tagging along with the professionals.

Somewhere through this Hellscape, lives were saved, and we will never know how many. I can tell you I saw people escaping the burning and the re-animates, making it to some kind of safety while everyone with a firehose and a weapon held off the nightmare.

What the guard and the cops did, what the firefighters did, it was insane. Holding the line against fire and the undead for people you will never know and never see again? Totally crazy.

And, dear God, it was the stuff of heroes.

Day Twenty

I was in downtown Miami this afternoon, where it feels like the re-animates have been taking over.

Two of them attacked a couple of people near an embankment. Both people were armed, but neither of them thought to aim for the head. Crazy, given the fact that people have been advised with every single broadcast to aim for the head. By now, we should all know that aiming anywhere else is worse than useless.

I wasn't much smarter. I had gone out unarmed, which was a bonehead move, and all I could do was yell "aim for the head! Aim for the head!"

Maybe those people couldn't hear me. I know from personal experience that if you don't wear earplugs, it only takes a couple of shots before your hearing isn't worth much for the next few hours. So, maybe those two people had been deafened by their own gunfire.

All I know is they put round after round into the bodies of the re-animates and they didn't stop until the undead were right on top of them.

After that, well, there wasn't much left ... and I got the hell out of there before anything could turn its attention to me.

That's the last time I leave the house without being armed.

Day Twenty-One

Biohazard signs have been appearing in Miami over the past month, warning of the risk of contagion from Argus/Jones. Some of those signs are posted at buildings that have grown emptier by the day. Every so often, you see signs defaced with the word "HOAX" or with some profanity. For the most part, though, people have left them alone.

People are trying, desperately trying, to behave as if containment still has a chance. Even though there is a state of emergency virtually everywhere, you see people doing their best to hold things together.

But I can feel the tension here, and I can sense something underneath it, something worse.

Fear.

It's as if there is a dam barely held in place and the cracks are beginning to show. When that dam breaks, it will cut loose explosively.

Day Twenty-Two

Photos and posters are now being posted in Miami, as people search for the missing and hold a vague hope that someone, somewhere, may have some word that can offer some shred of hope.

I can imagine the police, slammed as they are, have found it all but impossible to deal with what must be a flood of missing persons reports.

Often, the photos stapled to a utility pole or taped to any available surface represent that last grasping at straws, that search for some glimmer of news that may lead to the recovery of someone lost... or at least lead to some sort of closure.

I think of the image here. It's just a photo of two young women in happier times; one of many photos taped to a bulletin board of the missing. I found this photo, with a scrawled phone number and plea for contact, at a strip mall not far from downtown. I suspect that there are copies of this image posted everywhere in the city.

The note attached to this photo says the girls have been missing since early October, and it makes me wonder what may have happened to them since then.

Have these two vanished into a sea of missing persons? Were they overcome by the enemy that now stalks us all?

Or did their story have a happier conclusion?

I like to think that, perhaps, these two young women found their way home and are in some place safe with family and friends; that better times are a part of their future and not just a part of their past.

I know that thought is for my own consolation, but I prefer it to the darker roads my mind has taken lately.

Day Twenty-Three

Gunfire, blood, and sheets of rain tonight, and I know this is the end of things here.

The city of Miami has begun to die around me, as the dead hammer down the walls of the living and move in to take possession.

I feel as if I'm in the center of a Wagnerian opera or caught in a painting by Bosch. The crackle of shots, like a string of firecrackers ... the moaning of the dead who rise and walk just the same... the rise and fall of sirens like an audible tide.

Then, the stretches of silence ... and, oh, they are stretches that grow longer.

They scrape across the nerves.

I imagine other scenes, in other cities, all telling a story like this one. I imagine other people like me, telling of what they see as the cities around them fall ... I wonder what they may be writing ... I wonder if, before long, there will be anybody left to read...

Day Twenty-Four

In early September, barely a month ago, the population of the greater Miami area was more than six million souls.

Now, if there are six thousand left among the living, it will be nothing short of miraculous. The city, for all intents and purposes, has fallen to the dead.

Despite the best efforts to contain this new plague, city officials began a full evacuation of the remaining living people early this morning, just before dawn. Police, National Guard, and fire-rescue officials are all holding the rear-guard and covering the retreat.

In a day or so, I'll be leaving the city I've called home for my entire life, and I'll be striking out for the unknown.

We are being forced to leave this place and abandon our city ... our home ... to the undead.

Somebody had said the world would end October 21 this year.

He missed it by twenty-four hours.

Miami has fallen.

And the rest of the world is toppling along with it.

Day Twenty-Five

Yesterday things went to hell in Miami, and they've gone downhill from there.

I'd been planning to leave quietly during the weekend, but those plans got slapped down by life in the real world.

One hell of a time to neglect my annual flu shot ... and I'm paying for it.

Nights soaked in one fever dream after another, hard-pressed to tell if the scratching at the door is all in my mind, or if it comes from something that senses me and is scrabbling for a way in.

Last night was the worst. People I'd known, then forgotten, in a parade of faces half-decayed and just outside my window.

All a fever dream.

I can't make a decent move until I shake the worst of this. Maybe a few more days, and I'll be able to travel. Maybe a handful. But not more.

No television, except for the emergency broadcasts.

Late word had the interstate blocked in a solid mass. Luckily, I wasn't planning to head in that direction. I figured, rightly, the main roads would be the first to get overloaded. Maybe the flu bought me some time here. Time for the worst of the traffic to disperse.

Maybe some time to think more about my way out.

Sleep now. That's what I need. Rest.

Yes ... rest.

But no more dreams. Please, no more.

Day Thirty-Three
October 31
Halloween

A week and more of flu, fever dreams, and moments of delirium ... times when I was all but convinced that the episodes of the past month were nothing more than my imagination working through sweats hot and cold.

Not my imagination, after all. No fever.

And the light on my clock blinks late, so late, the night of October 31— the season of the dead; the dead who now know only hunger and nothing of the grave.

And more of sin and horror the soul of the plot, eh, Edgar Allan?

I can't help but wonder what Mr. Poe would have thought of nights like these.

Would he recoil at the sight of a loved one, long lost and now brought to some forgery of life? Would he wonder at the things that walk these shores, shambling wrecks from over that sea we were never meant to cross?

What would he think of the grave and its all-conquering worm, robbed of its conquest after all?

Would he shy away at the madness and horror? Or would he chronicle these days and charge the nightmare, journalist that he was, the writer and the old warhorse?

Is this nightmare challenge enough to draw the gentleman from his grave, or does he still rest peacefully while a skeletal hand places a rose and a bottle of cognac by that tombstone in Baltimore one more year...

Miami has grown dark now.

The sounds of traffic, of yelling and gunfire, of human cries that fall to low keening moans ... all have grown silent. Nothing stirs, not even the paper shambling of the dead.

The city has become a crypt.

Out are the lights, Mr. Poe.

Out all.

I will leave tomorrow.

Day Thirty-Four
Near The Border of Miami-Dade and Broward County, Florida
November 1

This was my first day on the road. I was able to travel a grand total of thirty miles before night closed in on me and I had to find some place that offered a degree of sanctuary.

Over the course of the day, I grew to treasure the rare stretches of clear roads like this one.

I'd made a good decision to stick with the back roads, but even then, I found myself doing a lot of weaving through the occasional jam of cars. Sometimes, obstacles forced me to backtrack and take another road altogether.

There were times when I could only measure my progress in the slow crawl of foot-by-foot travel.

Thankfully, the undead were rare, but I still kept my head on a swivel, jumping at the occasional shock when a dry crackle of a hand slapped against a window.

And I felt chills through the warmth of a south Florida afternoon in those moments when I found myself in the open — exposed and siphoning gasoline from the tanks of the dead cars around me.

I came to know intimately the sweat that gathered in my pits, that ran down my back or trickled down my temples, as the sun inched closer to the horizon with no safe place in sight.

The dead are worrisome enough during the day, but I can't shake the feeling that night gives them an edge; an advantage that makes cold, clammy fingers race up my back.

I don't know how much the re-animates depend on sight, but I swear it feels as if they become more aware of things when darkness falls.

In a darkened hotel, battery light shining from my laptop, I see the bones of the internet still up and alive as more of the infrastructure begins to fade away ... as the lights in the world blink out one by one.

Strange that this tiny corner of the world can still function when the rest begins to crumble.

December, Late
Broward County, Florida

We have come so far from where we were. Things that shook me those first days no longer make me blink, nor do they trouble my sleep. A change has worked its way on us. It is a ghastly thing, born of the charnel-house. For those of us still living, it's now the ordinary state of things.

The nature of the change, the sheer world-ending magnitude of it all, was driven home to me recently. The commonplace has become a thing that belongs to another century. That realization came to me in stark, uncompromising terms with a single event that spanned mere seconds.

Ironically, the event that was nearly my undoing was a thing that, in any other time, would have been insanely ordinary. As it was, the thing was damn near the end of me.

It all came down to a single misfortune born of my own carelessness. A foolish thing, and I hope I've learned from it. I had luck then, and I doubt I'll have that kind of luck again.

Now that I can think clearly and write again, I can piece together this account of welcome fortune and hopefully be the wiser for it.

November began with me leaving Miami, the city I've known as home.

Less than a week into that month, and still recovering from a bad case of the flu, I became one of the last casualties of a traffic accident.

It was stupid. A foolish thing. I have no idea what I was thinking, or if I was thinking at all. I had parked my car at a small hotel, paid for a night, then ran across the street to get a sandwich or something at the local convenience store.

I never checked the road.

There was the sound of a metal shriek, then something half-seen in the dusk, then a splintering crack. Then, darkness for a very long time.

But fortune favored the fool.

I was in a relatively out of the way place and refugees from the outbreaks had passed by this town without much of a thought.

There was no logistical or medical crisis in that place, at that time. There was no overwhelming need for medical services for the simple reason that many people had left this town for safer places. For weeks, I had an entire floor of a small hospital almost to myself.

The staff told me that I had run into the path of another car and had been thrown halfway down the street by the impact. And I was lucky, they said; luckier than any man should have been. The sum of all my injuries was a mild concussion, two broken legs, and a little skin left on the road.

I was very lucky. Even groggy from painkillers, I knew that much.

I had time to heal, and a place where I could.

I used my credit card to keep the hotel room, have the manager keep an eye on my car, and to pay off the bulk of my medical bills.

The hospital staff was very polite and professional about it all.

But I think we knew we were all just playing along, pretending that things hadn't changed all that much and that we would get back to the workings of the ordinary world before much longer.

Just pretending and playing the game.

But it was a good game, and it lasted maybe six weeks.

In December, near the middle part of the month, as nights even this far south begin to darken early, they cut the casts from my legs and sent me on my way.

I wasn't entirely ready. I needed at least another week in those casts, and we all knew it.

But we also knew we'd run out of time.

No more pretending, not for any of us.

The infection had reached this small town, and the hospital was now becoming crowded with the sick and the dying.

And, on the other end of death, there were the moans and the keenings; the leathery straining at restraints.

The sounds of the animated dead had begun to infiltrate the hospital, their noise accentuating the growing silence where once were brisk steps and crisp voices over the intercom.

On crutches, and with a warning to take it easy for as long as I could, I was released by a reluctant doctor into a world where I might or might not live long enough to mend.

On unsteady legs, I made my way back to my hotel.

My car was still there, with nothing disturbed.

The door to my room opened to my touch. Inside, everything was covered in dust. There was a general air of disuse about the place; a sense of a place abandoned.

Not even the undead were there.

Along my painful trip back to the hotel, and as I settled in my room, there was no sign or sound of either the living or the undead. My sanctuary was undisturbed.

I spent a week there, slowly learning how to walk again.

I left the day after I found the body of the manager.

The man was seated at the front desk, leaning back slightly in his chair. He had a bite wound on his arm, and a single gunshot wound to the side of his head. His mummy-like hand still held his pistol.

I rolled the man back to his living quarters, pulling him along in his chair. I then moved him onto his bed, crossing his arms over his chest. I could have left him where I found him, but the idea just felt wrong. Putting him to rest seemed like the decent thing, the human thing, to do. I couldn't even bring myself to take his gun. I left him there, hopefully in peace.

When I got back to my car, I checked my provisions and other supplies, turned on the ignition, and began the drive toward Orlando. I stuck with my decision to stay with the back roads as I began to make my way out of the state.

The hotel calendar said it was Christmas Eve.

December 25

Broward County, Florida

Atomic clocks and the batteries of our countless devices keep faithful time and even update our machines with a cool regularity. But is there anyone left to note the passing of the hours?

Technology works in starts and fits. I am recharging all my batteries in an abandoned hotel where the power still flows.

Tomorrow, some phantom turbine somewhere may seize up, or it may sputter and spin down.

Electricity is fickle now. It seems to come and go whenever it has a mind to do so.

Christmas Day was like that.

I kept myself holed up in a hotel room, not far from the outskirts of West Palm Beach, and along the back roads that parallel Interstate 95.

The chime of church bells, tolling the morning, threw me from bed with a jack-rabbit start.

The sound seemed to fill the empty morning and roll back down the streets in long and desolate echoes.

And then the tide of moans.

Empty husks of voices, drawn from dead throats and the wheeze of tattered lungs.

A litany of the dead. And I wondered what the churchmen might think of that. What, in their season, might they make of a world where the dead walk and answer sound with reflex sound.

And the morning was warm, but I shivered all the same.

Late December
Late Word from Tokyo

I learned that Japan fell today.

I received a garbled account from Tokyo of a mob attacking a local commuter train.

The person who sent the account sent something fragmented and hard to make out ... heavy packet and information loss from their end, I suppose.

It's a wonder anything got through at all.

I was given bits and pieces of a nation fighting a retreating battle against the onslaught of the dead; the sense that the technological giant was beginning its fall with a nightmare slowness.

The author left me with the sense that the end for Japan, as a global power ... perhaps as a civilization that is among Earth's oldest ... is but a breath and a cold clutch away.

The narrative, for all the broken English and shards of data, is a familiar one.

It is the same story I saw outside my apartment window in Miami; the undead as a crawling tide that slowly drowns out all life.

The tale, though so very familiar to me, has not lost its power to chill.

Here, as the year draws to a close and a deeper level of night descends on us, I wonder at what may be happening on that far side of this world.

Have the people of Japan found refuge in old mountain redoubts? Does an element of that old civilization still survive? Will that nation and its people stand?

Or has the land of the rising sun fallen to the night without end?

December 31
Palm Beach County, Florida

New Year's Eve, and a time of greater changes is upon me now.

When I first left Miami, I had hoped to make my way to Atlanta and the presumed safety of the Centers for Disease Control. Now I have learned that, if I ever hope to find some safe haven, I need to look somewhere else.

I had been scouring the internet for some crumbs of news, and any indication that this plague might be on the verge of breaking. Instead, the news dashed my hopes of refuge near Atlanta.

One of the last reports I was able to salvage brought the grim news. The CDC had been compromised and was locked down; presumed lost. One of the last bastions in the fight against this plague had fallen.

And so, my travel plans must change.

As I work to prepare myself to exist in a world changed beyond recognition, I must be ready for a journey that will be longer and more hazardous than first expected.

Gone is the safe horizon of Atlanta, gone down to ashes and the dark scrabbling of the undead. I must strike out for a new destination.

I trace my new route along paper maps I scavenged from back-road service stations; maps that are relics of an older time.

Under the guidance of battery-powered lamplight, my finger traces a path to my new destination: Colorado.

I will follow the roads from Florida across the Gulf States, then north to my destination.

I'll go to Cheyenne Mountain, and perhaps the last human outpost on this continent.

My journey begins on the first day of the new year.

January 2
Palm Beach County, Florida

I began my journey from Florida yesterday, planning to reach the state of Colorado by late spring or early summer. The road to those good intentions, I have found, is paved with the wreckage of cars and a vast overestimation of my own skills.

In other words, I had almost no clue how weak I still am. Once again, good fortune was all that kept my own stubbornness from killing me.

I was able to find shelter in one of the small bedroom towns along the back roads from Palm Beach County, and I know I'll need to stay here for a while and get back to my full strength ... or something close to it.

Truthfully, I like my sanctuary. It's a common enough looking community. Anonymous and all but impossible to discern from thousands like it.

Silent, vague, and so generic that even now the eye slides past it.

Places like this were best known for being so completely like each other that a person could move from one community to another halfway across the country and not notice any difference. It feels as if all the years of ranked anonymity seeped into the pores of the brick and stonework; after all the ages, the buildings learned the art of being unseen and unremarked.

Curiously, in my time here, even the dead have given this place no notice.

I'd be tempted to stay here, except that even in my weakened condition, I am driven to reach Colorado. I need to learn, to see with my own eyes, whether other pockets of survivors exist.

But this anonymous, pastel community is so very tempting.

Water can be found within easy reach, and food can be grown.

Seedlings from an abandoned garden store not far away have taken root already.

It might have been a good home ... in a world where the dead kept to their graves.

But I know better.

This place is a brief sanctuary, and only that.

Soon, I must move on. It's either that or wait for death to find its shambling way to me.

January 10
Palm Beach County, Florida
Shave and a Haircut, My Two Bits

I regarded the face in the mirror with a mixture of interest and healthy suspicion. It was my face, but I'd never seen it like this before. I'd shaved my head and whiskers as a concession to the uncertainty of cleanliness in this new world. Put another way, I wanted to make sure that my scalp and ... other areas ... didn't become homes for fleas or other six-legged wildlife. I wanted to play it safe till I knew for sure that I had been keeping clean enough to discourage any uninvited guests. So, gone is every hair on my head and everywhere else, including my mustache. I'm keeping the eyebrows, though.

I used clippers that I pillaged from a barbershop where people kept something held over from the old days. These are manual clippers. They do a good job of keeping hair tidy, and they can be adjusted for a buzz cut. After that, all it takes is a few swipes with a razor to shave everything else and, voila, I look like a cue ball.

My face has become a bit thinner than I remember it, thanks to my time in the hospital, but it's a long way from being gaunt. It's the shaven scalp that bothers me. It doesn't feel like it fits. Maybe I was expecting to sport a look that was somewhere between avant-garde and supervillain, and what I got was a look that screams "plain and ordinary."

I'm still not sure I like this look, but I console myself with the knowledge that it'll keep me clean until I know for sure that I can manage without having to worry about bugs that bite. I've also been cheered by the fact that no talent scout for a beauty contest will be around to glare askance at me.

I looked in the mirror, rubbed my shaven scalp, and cocked an eyebrow.

"So, we meet again, detective. But this time the advantage is mine."

Nope, that is not gonna work, not even with a stylish East European accent. So much for a potential career as an evil genius.

I muttered to myself as I packed my clippers, thinking about how all the TV shows and comic books lied to me.

February
Palm Beach County, Florida

I connected my computer to the Internet, learning this is the second week of February. Surprised to see the Internet still working, but feeling a little better for finding out. I'd like to hope that this is a good sign, but a look at a couple of popular social media sites doesn't offer much encouragement there.

In fact, the fragmented messages from the popular sites are few, far between, old ... and pretty blood-chilling.

There were a couple that stood out, though. One was from somewhere in the Mid-West.

"Been watching my neighbor's house. They've ... hiding in there since things started. The other day, he hurt his hand. Cut it on some barbed wire ... It had caught one of those things. The thing was still there ... struggling in the wire. Neighbor got its blood in his cut. Not good. He looked scared. Next morning ... said he wasn't feeling well. Went to go take a nap, he said. Last night it didn't sound good in the house. Wife ... screaming like she was being attacked by something. Today, I haven't seen either of them and things there are too quiet. The neighborhood no longer feels safe. It feels too scary to stay. Gotta find a way to get out of the city. I'm starting to run out of food, too. Better leave while I can ..."

The other message fragment came from somewhere near northern California, and it was an audio message fragmented almost to the point of being indecipherable. This was the best I could make of it.

"Desperate now ... reach basement ... Keep ... food back there ... Hiding ... nobody to find it ... just me ...Something ... there! I can't see ... too dark ... But it's there ... the shadows ... it waits ... batteries weak ... lamps dim ... dying ... Must turn away, leave ... But I can't

... so hungry ... must reach the food ... should never have kept it ... basement ... Something is moving ... "

I have tried to reply to these messages.

There has been no response, no other contact.

Only silence.

A pair of cautionary tales for those of us who remain.

These messages are warnings that we all need to be extremely careful. The safe place of the moment can be compromised, with terrible consequences.

We are no longer the apex predator in this world. We have been replaced by something that is persistent and so very patient; something that can hide in the shadows or broad daylight with alarming ease.

Something that will never fear death.

March

An Interlude

It is strange to be entering data into this page, uploading it to what remains of the Internet, wondering if there is anyone out there who may see what I write ... or if my words are being sent to an empty sky; a phantom architecture where no living eyes remain to bear witness. But I have, if not hope, at least something. Let's call it a stubborn determination and leave it at that.

Either way, I've chosen to write and summon the ghosts of the Internet. I will continue to call down the magic of the wireless and etch the symbols of hyperlink and plain text into my sendings. I will cast them to the far reaches of that electrified space that may yet be preserved and without decay.

I won't be above sending out some practical advice when I learn a better way to do things, either.

Case in point: before reaching Orlando, I learned there's a better way to charge batteries. Use a set of reduction gears. These save a great deal of work, can be carried in a backpack, and can be found at your local hardware store. Get a bicycle, hook up the gears to a wheel, tie the whole mess to your charger, and presto. Peddle and charge. It's still work, but, with a little practice, it's fast work, and you can charge damn near anything.

It's insanely easy to find this equipment once you know to look for it. I found mine at a store that had been looted of just about everything but practical items. For some reason, if an item or a set of tools looks like something involving work, looters will avoid it almost every time.

That's the thing about looters, bless their short-sighted hearts. They almost always grab the expensive and fancy stuff while neglecting the simple things that could have saved their lives. Every store that sells high technology is usually a gutted wreck, emptied of high-end appliances that nobody will be able to use again for a very long time. Go to the backrooms of those same businesses and you'll find plenty of serviceable equipment sitting at the workbench.

I advise you, in that spirit, to keep an eye out for the occasional odd items that are more about manual work and less about modern convenience. A hammer and a few handfuls of nails will serve you better than a high-tech nail-gun. Hammers don't run out of juice.

Anything that connects to a household outlet is going to be worse than useless. Of course, that hasn't stopped the local looters, the same people who keep stealing those big-screen TVs. They keep at it and I have yet to see any situation where they've made the connection between an absence of electricity and cool appliances that mysteriously don't work.

Sorry, Internet. No cat pictures today, only survival instructions.

Late March, and Orlando

I arrived in Orlando as Florida's winter calendar turned toward spring, and this city is where my last wild hope came to die.

Despite mountains of evidence to the contrary, I had clung to that faint hope that there might be some signs that a community was holding on, surviving in the face of the plague of the undead. Maybe there was something that remained, by chance or miracle. I had clutched at those hopes the way a drowning person will clutch at anything that offers even the most outlandish chance of survival.

Cancel those hopes and bury them with the dead; there is no safe haven here and no straws for the drowning man to grasp.

Orlando is gone — abandoned and left to the re-animates.

As nearly as I can tell, there was no protracted fight here, such as I saw in Miami; no case of ground being lost one inch at a time to the re-animates in their relentless advance.

By every measure I could figure, Orlando was the subject of a hasty but organized evacuation. Barriers in the city appeared to offer nothing more than token resistance; meant more to delay the advance of the undead than to repel them entirely.

Inside the city, there was nothing to find but the leathery shuffling of feet as the dead wandered the streets aimlessly. They were once living people in a living city. Now they are vacant bodies, without goal or motive.

From the shadows, holding my breath, I watched from the safest distance I could manage. The dead were few here and scattered. Still, I know that an unaware turn can lead from an empty street into confrontation, and the gaze of sightless eyes.

I navigated the city with safety.

Those were the sensations and impressions that dogged me like shadows for two days and two restless nights in the city.

Enough time to know nothing remained for me here.

Checking the approaches to Orlando, I was able to determine that the Interstate was clear ... nothing as far as could be seen.

I took my notes, then siphoned enough fuel to top off my car.

It was time to leave Florida.

Driving through the city outskirts, I saw the sun gleaming on buildings that already seemed to be growing dull with a sense of disuse.

The moaning of the dead was a dirge at my back.

April
On the Road

Orlando is now long behind me now, though its memory won't leave me alone.

I left the city with a host of conflicting feelings jostling for my attention: relief that I was putting behind another enclave of the dead; regret that I could find none of the living; sorrow that a city once so alive was now empty ... as vacant of life as the creatures that shambled its streets.

It was surreal to drive the empty roads leading out of Orlando. Areas once packed with traffic were barren of any active transport. I saw little beside the occasional burnt-out vehicle resting charred and dead by the side of the road.

Interstate 4 was the lone exception. That ribbon of highway that winds through the core of the city was still choked with traffic. But nothing was moving. There was no blare of horns, no voices shouting over the din of traffic. There was only the silence of things abandoned.

It was as if all humanity had just disappeared overnight, leaving nothing but its artifacts.

Stores, parks, and cityscapes built by generations of humanity are all that remain. They are empty, all of them.

Of the builders there is no longer any sign.

As I passed the occasional vehicle, I faced the fact that it's only going to be a matter of time before something, whether a shortage of fuel or a road rendered impassable, forces me to abandon my car and to leave behind one more piece of the world I knew.

The time is coming when I'll need to remove my bike from its rack on this car, or the next one ... and set out with nothing but the possessions I can carry. That is no abstract thought. That is a very real event; a thing that will happen. The only question is when.

I'm surprised by how calmly I consider these things — the prospect of leaving my car and of surviving in a wilderness populated by the undead.

The worst has already happened. If there are nightmares ahead, they won't be more terrible.

They'll only be different.

Late April
Near Gainesville
Securing a King's Ransom

I'm still on track to get to Colorado and I'm working to time my arrival by early fall. If I can get there by the end of October, then I'll have bought enough time to find winter shelter ... just in case Cheyenne Mountain has fallen along with everything else.

My planned route gets me out of Florida in another month, then through the back roads of the Gulf states and up through Texas and the Oklahoma panhandle. That'll get me into Colorado with time to spare.

It gives me time to build a few things along the way.

And I reflect on an expression that was archaic when I was a child: "Worth a King's Ransom."

The expression draws its roots from the days when prisoners of war who belonged to a high estate were, when imprisoned, released for a great sum of money or other treasure ... a ransom.

Now, the ransom is not to be found in gold, jewels, or deeds to land. Now, the treasures reside in the memories of those who would rebuild. They may also be found between the pages of books. There is wealth enough to recover from the brink, wealth enough to haul knowledge from out of the dark ages, wealth enough to rebuild a civilization.

It's a King's Ransom, if ever there was one.

All we need are the books, carefully preserved, and enough of the living to read them.

I cannot guarantee the second, but I have begun work on the first.

In the empty towns that I visit, I seek out the book and hardware stores.

Books are collected and sealed within cocoons of plastic weave. Plastic bags and silicon beads complete the packaging, then all is wrapped in another layer of heavy plastic wrapping.

I am using everything I know to preserve the texts.

Where it's possible, I add a computer to the package. The battery is carefully removed, and a hand-charger is placed within the package.

Physical media, mostly collections of discs, carry the higher information such as chemistry and physics and history and astrophysics.

And I include literature and letters. I want to safeguard the voices of those long gone, who wrote of worlds real and imaginary with a breathtaking sweep.

Lincoln's and Washington's words are preserved in these discs, alongside the words of Lao Tsu and Julius Caesar.

Homeric Odysseys and the works of Shakespeare are bookended with travels through lands of high fantasy.

The print books are the blueprints for keeping a civilization alive. They cover the basics: everything from gardening to woodcraft to how to build or repair a shelter. I've included subjects as simple as water purification and fire-building, and as complex as first aid and battlefield medicine.

I have enclosed the basics of math and how to tell time by the sun and stars. Truthfully, I've added everything I can imagine when it comes to keeping a community alive.

There is even a selection of books that teach younger people how to read. That is my sole concession to optimism ... the hope that enough survive, and find these works, leading a new generation to be taught to read and to rebuild.

I've packed discs that preserve the things that give life dimension; that remind us that the stars were once within our reach and may be again.

These caches, these King's Ransoms, are being left in the places I visit, the survival stacks clearly marked and labeled for those who may find them.

One town, one village, one city at a time, I leave these markers and all this wealth.

I give these riches freely to all who would use them ... and one day light the cities again.

May
A Hasty Memorial Near Pensacola

Now on the outskirts of a small town near Pensacola, and there was a scene that will stay with me. A poignant set-piece that is both tragic and profound. I hope I never forget it.

I was taking my westward track out of Florida, following the back roads, and stopping only to search for supplies or build one of the small caches I try to leave whenever I can collect books and simple tools, leaving all of it in carefully weather-proofed piles.

I stumbled on the scene almost by accident. It was in a shaded roadside area, in a place that would have been unremarkable in other times.

I came across seven filled graves, and one empty one. Beside the graves, I found the desiccated corpse of a man, dressed in the forest camouflage familiar to the US Army.

The body of the man was seated, in erect posture, under a tree close to the graves. Beside him, eight packs were arranged in a neat double row, protected by a plastic sheet.

The man sat with the barrel of a rifle under his chin. He had used the weapon to fire a single bullet into his brain.

He had left a handwritten note and a set of seven dog tags beside him. Everything was bundled in plastic and held in place by a rock. It was all done with great precision and extraordinary care.

Nothing had been touched or disturbed in any way. I was the first living thing to come upon this scene.

Reading the note, I learned that the soldier was the leader of a squad belonging to the Army National Guard. He and his team had been instructed to make a quick sweep of a grouping of small towns.

It was part of an effort to locate any of the living ... and to eliminate any of the dead.

These men did nothing wrong, nothing foolish. They were professionals who were undone by that most freakish of accidents.

While investigating a wrecked medical vehicle, the guardsmen found a case of glass vials filled with contaminated blood ... vials that had been exposed to the unfiltered sun for just a moment too long. The pressures of gasses, building inside the vials, finally caused them to rupture explosively.

The guardsmen opened the case at that very moment.

They were sprayed with a hail of glass shards and contaminated with the blood of the re-animates.

They chose death rather than to wait for what they all knew would happen.

The eighth guardsman buried his friends, then went about the job of collecting their gear and arranging it as I had found it.

The note instructed "whoever finds this" to take what they could use, just "make sure the tags find their way home."

I chose one of the military grade rifles, finding ammunition and a manual on how to use it ... breathing a silent thanks that the soldier had considered the prospect of an untrained civilian stumbling across it.

I was also able to find two sets of camouflage clothing that fit me, as well as a pair of durable boots and some heavy socks.

Rations, a compass, water purification tablets and other gear made it into my pack and saddlebags ... all secured in my car.

Before leaving, I took the last set of dog tags and filled the last grave.

Rest well, soldier.

If I can deliver these tags, then I'll do that. And I'll bring your story with me.

I will let the living know that you died well and would have made them proud.

Late May
A Memento at Mobile Bay

I found another photo today. This one was tacked to a bulletin board in a small-town square. A weathered thing, nearly transparent, sharing space with so many other photos like it. They had completely crowded out the usual papers and leaflets, the advertisements for services, offers of items for sale, and a thousand other casual notices that crowded these boards.

One overriding search, that for missing people, displaced all others.

A note, in thin pencil scrawl, was taped to the bottom of the photo. It asked if anyone had seen the two men in the image, identified only as "Jim" and "Terry."

Just one of thousands of similar photos, all asking the same question ... all looking for those who had gone missing. It reminded me of the first such image I had seen, in Miami, at the plague's outbreak. That posting had sought the safe return of two ordinary young women. Now, someone was searching for two ordinary young men.

In the tattered, weathered photo, I could sense the hope for information, the hope for a person's safe return.

I wonder if anyone in this image ever found their way home. Or if the photograph is all that remains of them.

June
Alabama
The Bandits

I ran across a couple of opportunists today. I suppose a better description might have been 'bandits,' or 'robbers,' or 'low-life predatory assholes.' Regardless of the descriptions ... and I prefer the last one ... they were both united in a single purpose: to take advantage of anyone weaker than they were.

I had parked my car nearby and was scouting the area on foot. I wasn't looking for anything more than an assurance that the road ahead was going to be structurally safe. I'd come up against a couple of wash-outs recently, so I found the occasional long-range check to be a good idea. Besides, it was nice to get out of the car and stretch my legs from time to time.

I heard the voices of the bandits as I turned a bend in the road so I slowed down, practiced the fine art of keeping out of sight, and approached the voices for a better look. I unshipped my binoculars as soon as I reached a place where I could see and not be seen.

The bandits hadn't heard my car and that was something that surprised me. Gasoline engines aren't designed for stealth, and when your car is the only one on the road it makes the engine sound all the louder. The bandits, however, had been focused on what they were doing: laughing and joking as they looted the occupants of a wrecked SUV.

The car had crashed into a concrete barrier, probably one of several that had been set up along the road to help facilitate a mass migration out of Pensacola. Even looking through my binoculars, I couldn't tell how long ago the crash had been or if it had killed all of the vehicle's occupants. Had some escaped? That was hard to say, but it looked like there were at least two dead people in the car.

The bandits had pried open the doors and spilled everything from the car into the road. They had been stripping the corpses of valuables, cackling and gleefully going through their loot when low, whistling moans caught their attention. I knew those moans all too well. Those were the sounds made by re-animates.

Both of the bandits jerked their heads up at the same time and I could have sworn that I saw their eyes bug out in surprise. I tracked their line of sight through my field glasses and saw what had them panicked. I counted six re-animates shambling toward the bandits, who had lost all focus on their surroundings. They'd been so busy playing pirate that they had left their guns out of reach. There were now two re-animates between the men and their weapons, and more of the undead were coming.

From the looks of things, the bandits had screwed themselves thoroughly.

One of the guys, however, managed to show a glimmer of intelligence. He picked up a rock and lobbed it toward a pick-up truck. The sound of the rock rattling around in the metal truck bed was enough to draw the attention of the re-animates, and that bought the bandits enough time to get to their guns.

I put away my binoculars and watched the bandits, their composure recovered, methodically shoot the re-animates. I was impressed with their skill as they aimed with great care and put one round after another through the heads of the undead. Not a single shot went to waste. It made me glad that I was at a safe distance from those guys and completely out of their sight.

I would have stood and applauded the bandits for their marksmanship, but I was now looking at them through the scope of my rifle, so my hands were otherwise occupied. Besides, I was utterly focused on making sure my aim was solid. I tracked each of the bandits carefully before I committed to pulling the trigger. If I missed either shot, my level of risk would quickly get into dangerous territory.

Satisfied with my aim, I squeezed the trigger and took out the first bandit, hitting him squarely in the back. The second man spun around looking for the source of the shot. He went down with a round to the chest. I watched the two men through my scope, making sure they were as dead as the re-animates they had put down. I listened for any other sounds, either living people or re-animates who might have been drawn by the gunfire. I heard nothing, so I went back to my car and prepared to drive on.

I had taken two human lives and I didn't feel a shred of remorse over it. I knew I had done the safe thing and the smart thing. Maybe the right thing. If I had let these two men go, there was every chance that they would have ambushed me or someone else somewhere down the road. That was a chance I didn't want to take.

Ironically, it was the sight of the two men looting the dead in that car that changed my mind about them. There is something unsettling about grave-robbers. It takes a special kind of cold calculation to steal from corpses. It raises my hackles and tells me these people pose a danger to the living, too. I have no compunction about ending that kind of person.

Honestly, if I'd seen these same two guys breaking into a store, I'd have given them a pass. A certain level of breaking and entering is fast becoming a way of life. It's no big deal as far as I'm concerned. And shoplifting? Please! I've ransacked more than a few stores lately without leaving money on the counter, so I'm not going to judge someone else whose only crime is trying to stay alive and not hurt anybody.

Robbing the dead and laughing while you do it? That's where I draw the line. Oh, maybe these two bandits would never have bothered me or another living soul. Maybe they would have been content simply to rifle through cars and steal from corpses and let it go at that.

Maybe not.

All I could know for sure was that they weren't going to bother the living now. If they were ever going to be a threat, that threat had been removed.

I knew I would sleep better for it.

June
Little Luxuries

I find myself in a reflective mood today.

I'm thinking about some of the luxuries we have, which are things we never used to give a second thought. I doubt we ever took anything so for granted as we did our technology ... and the older the tech, the less we noticed it.

I'd just crossed into Alabama when I got reacquainted with one of the simplest of luxuries ... a warm-water shower.

It was a day after a raid on a small camping store. I found one of those "disposable" kits for a camp shower. An easy principle: fill the bag with water, hang it in direct sunlight, and let Sol do the rest.

The bag looked like one of the ever-present artifacts of our earlier age: durable, yet still disposable with no great hardship incurred. Not any more. Now, if you find something like this, you keep it and be thankful for having it.

I did as the bag instructed and spent my day checking my supplies. What did I need? What did I have? What had been used beyond my capacity to repair? The serviceable items were carefully repacked, and the worn-out items were carefully buried, and the soil made to look undisturbed.

For some reason, even in these early days, I feel it's best to leave as few clues to my campsites as possible. I've left caches of books, tools, and some supplies in the towns I pass through, but those are designed to be found.

I'm a bit more circumspect with my own footprints.

Work done, I returned to the moment.

The splash of warm water brought back a flood of memories: of a time when there was electricity and air-conditioning; of the smell of soap and the crisp feel of freshly washed clothes ... or a hot meal cooked and eaten while watching or ignoring whatever was on television.

Of a time when the line of demarcation between life and death was definite and clear.

It is a strange trick of perspective for me; a sense of double vision or world overlay. I walk in one world but carry the memories of another. They are the memories of a world gone for perhaps less than a year, yet as out of reach as Ancient Rome.

July? August, Maybe?

I seem to have lost track of time.

When I began this journal, I felt confident that, worst case, I'd be in Atlanta before the end of the summer.

Then, Colorado by the middle of fall.

Now? I'm not sure.

I thought the calendar in my computer would help me keep track of time. If that didn't work, I was sure I'd know how to tell the passing of time by the constellations in the night sky.

Yeah. About that.

The nights are filled with stars, and that's my problem. There are too many. I can't pick out the more prominent constellations. I'm not that good at knowing where to look. Light pollution used to be the bane of amateur astronomers, and now the clear nights with their abundance of stars have become reminders that I'm not as smart as I thought I was. On a good night, I can pick out the Big Dipper and Orion, and that's about it. I couldn't tell you what their positions in the night sky mean if my life depended on it.

I still have my trusty compass and my paper maps to keep me from being completely lost, but it looks like I'm not gonna get that Junior Woodsman merit badge, after all.

And my technical skills aren't exactly shining examples, either. My computer's internal calendar tells me it's June, then decides it's July, August, November, take your pick. Never the same month on two consecutive days, and I have yet to figure out a way to troubleshoot the thing.

The remnants of the Internet are just as unreliable, but at least there is something functioning there. I can still upload these entries from my journal. If you're reading this one, I hope you know more about what day it is than I do.

All I know for sure is that I'm traveling along the Alabama cost and it feels like late summer. I'm not entirely sure of the month, and shame on me for letting my attention slip.

I'm confident that I haven't lost track of too many days. It's probably just a couple of days into July, maybe a week at most. The problem is with my laptop's internal clock, which I don't know how to fix without the comfort of a stack of technical manuals and maybe a crash course in coding.

I'll keep an eye out for another machine with the next town I visit. Once I get another laptop, I'll feel better about either tinkering with this one or transferring my data to the new machine. The last thing I want to do is to fry this computer while I'm trying to fix it.

If it comes down to it, I'll just keep track of time by counting the sunsets and marking them on another page here. It may mean that I'll be off by a couple of weeks in my date-keeping, but I can deal with that.

I'd rather be off by a week or two than short out my only means of taking notes.

Late July
Mississippi
The Attack

I am here to write these words and I wish I could credit that to my skill.

But it was luck, every bit of it; and if luck was a checking account, I'd be seriously overdrawn by now.

God, where to begin?

I had just crossed the Alabama state line and was traveling into Mississippi, sticking to my back roads, when my car finally gave out.

I'd been expecting that. Wrecked vehicles had been getting scarcer, and those I could find were nothing more than stalled-out hulks with their gas tanks bone dry. I'd had the devil's own time finding anything that still had some gas to siphon.

Add to those difficulties the increasingly uneven sounds my engine was making. I could tell that I'd been getting a liberal mix of gasoline and water with every fill-up. That's just the sort of thing to mess up a car.

Oddly enough, it wasn't the bad gasoline that finally killed my vehicle. It was the lack of oil. I'd noticed a small leak; the sort of thing that you can delay fixing as long as you have a spare can of the stuff to dump into the engine from time to time. I could tell from a couple of empty cans in the back seat that the car's previous owner must have known that and was planning to get things fixed "one of these days."

Only that day never came.

I was aware this was something that needed watching, and I had tried my hand at prevention. I'd even attempted to drain a few oil pans to buy my car a little more time, but the stuff that dribbled out was a sludgy mess that would have just gummed things up.

So I limped along in this car, hoping I could find one in better shape.

Only *that* day never came, either. And, one day, my car sputtered and smoked and seized up.

And that was the end of things for my latest and last set of wheels.

But, like I said, I had been expecting something like this from day one, and I'd prepared for it. Along the way I'd even had the bright idea to make a travois and add a pair of wheels to it so I could carry more than just what was in my pack.

I took the bike down from its rack on the back of the car, got my pack, saddlebags, and everything I could pile on the travois, and set off down the road.

This is the part where I made my most dangerous mistake.

I'd gotten accustomed to the undead around me and had stopped paying close attention to them.

You'd think that, of all the mistakes to cut short a life, this would top the list.

But here's the thing.

Through my travels along the roadways, the re-animates were always strapped into their cars. They might slap at the windows with leather hands or snap at me with jagged teeth the color of old ivory, but they couldn't work a seatbelt or open a car door. They were trapped by passive restraints and simple latches they could no longer use or understand.

Reflex took over for me. I learned to ignore them. Like a complete idiot.

I was peddling through a small cluster of shops, more a wide place in the road than a true border town, when the wheels on my travois started squeaking. They weren't making much of a noise, so I figured I had time to find a hardware store and get a can of lubricant.

I wasn't thinking about the fact that the undead can be drawn by sound.

And I wasn't thinking about the fact that not all the re-animates were stuck inside cars.

Or that they could come from anywhere.

My first clue was the sound of low, whistling moans as two re-animates shuffled into the road in front to me and turned to face me.

I stopped my bike, dropped the kickstand, and unlimbered my rifle. I took careful aim as the re-animates continued shuffling toward me, waiting for them to get close enough for a good shot.

Then I heard a moan from behind me, close enough to raise the hairs on my neck.

I spun around as fast as I could and, God, it was a near thing. He was almost on top of me. I barely had time for a single shot. There was absolutely no time for anything else. No time to do anything but aim and hope my practicing was going to pay off.

I didn't even have time to get ear plugs, or to remember that I'd need them.

It was a clear shot, point-blank, and it shattered the re-animate's skull into powder. It also made my ears ring like church bells.

I couldn't hear the moans of the two undead who had been in front of me, or the moaning of those now drawn by my gunfire.

I took out the two re-animates I had first seen, knowing my hearing was going to be a lost cause for the next few hours. By that time, I could see that maybe a half dozen re-animates were closing in on me from different directions, and more probably were coming.

And, dear God, I could see motion in the trees behind the storefronts. Re-animates were moving. They had remained still and silent for so long that vines had grown up around them, and now they were on the move. It looked like corpses were literally melting out from the woods.

I was surrounded and, with my hearing as muffled as it was, I had no way of knowing how many of these things were coming or how close they were. One of them could be behind me, and I'd never know.

I spun around and around, feeling the trap close, looking for some way out, any way out.

I got lucky.

I saw a storefront with its window completely intact. My first shot shattered the window. My second brought down a set of shelves, which must have started a chain reaction among the other shelves and items that were stacked or scattered nearby. The whole thing must have made an unholy racket, because every re-animate that had been coming my way turned and started shambling toward that store.

I stayed still, and silent. I didn't dare move until I saw a clear path out.

And when I moved, I moved with a painful slowness, breathing silently though my mouth and praying to something, anything, that I wouldn't betray myself with a sound.

I left that town, moving inch by inch and silently thanking every agent of luck and providence I could think of.

It was nightfall by the time I reached the edge of town, but I kept my slow pace until daybreak.

When I knew I was in the clear, I got back on my bicycle and rode through the rest of the day.

With nightfall, I scouted a place where I could make a camp.

I searched for any of the undead first, making very sure the area was clear.

I could see some buildings in the distance.

I made no move to go near them.

August

Mississippi

An Encounter with the Insane

I had to kill a person today.

This was not one of the re-animates or one of the barely human scavengers I have encountered on, thankfully, rare occasions. This was a living, breathing woman.

In another world she might have been beautiful.

In this world, her features were twisted by a chilling shape of madness, and a reminder that the dead are not always the things to fear.

I had heard of cases like this one from reports early in the outbreak, before I abandoned Miami, but this was my first personal encounter with one of these people. Sometimes they are solitary, sometimes they move in groups, but they always share a common pathology. They will wear fancy dress and douse themselves with paint, ketchup, syrup ... anything the color of rusted blood.

Alone or in groups, they laugh and shriek.

All of them are turning, dancing to the unheard rhythm of a lunatic pulse ...

And nothing of reason is left in the burning lanterns of their eyes.

The riot of expression is the mark of their long fall into madness.

This woman bore the same mark as all the others. She was one of the legion whose minds had cracked from their hinges, who had given themselves up to the costumed trappings of the living dead.

But where the eyes of the undead are gray, filmy things and vacant; where the motions of the re-animates are the motions of the decrepit, in the madness of the living there is a hectic excess of expression.

Motions are extravagant; convulsive. Laughter is loud, racing up the scale to an ear-splitting crescendo.

There is no gatekeeper here; no reason to temper actions or vocalizations.

And that is the thing that makes these people more dangerous than the dead.

The commotion draws the re-animates, and these people do not flinch from them.

The danger to others is disturbingly clear.

The person is living, but insane. They have no regard for their safety, or your own. They will laugh, and dance a riotous dance and fill the air with raucous noise. And they will draw the dead, in all their numbers, right to you.

Do you try to save the living person with the empty mind and risk what you know is coming? Do you hope against thin hope that you might be able to do the impossible before this person's howls and shrieks of madness summon a crowd of the undead, before that crowd tightens around you and ends all chance of escape?

Or do you do the unthinkable?

In another time, there might be room to treat these people ... to bring them back from the place they occupy now ... to reawaken the light of sane humanity in those eyes.

But it has been a long time since we had that luxury.

You do the unthinkable. You dispatch these living just as you would dispatch the dead.

I took a long look at the person dancing ever closer to me, shrieking and cackling. I looked into the eyes of the woman who might have been beautiful, in another place. Another time. Then I raised my rifle, aimed, and fired a single shot into her still-beating heart.

And that was that, and it was so brutally simple. Just point. And shoot. And try to forget what you just did.

And so, the dead claim another victory over us.

If I believed them capable of thought, I would call it an insidious design. We are compelled, in fighting the dead, to turn our weapons on some of the living.

In a world where life is scarce already, we must kill some of our own ... without choice, without option.

God help us, without hesitation.

August
Thoughts on Paradox, History, and Motion at the Speed of Death

The undead are a paradox.

I grant you, it should be a thing that goes without saying. I mean, let's face it, the entire notion of the dead walking the earth and not politely staying in their coffins or their graves is one that is counterintuitive right out of the gate.

Yet here we are.

No, the paradox has to do with their behavior. I will confess on these pages and in this place that it's a thing that nags at me and keeps me thinking through sleepless nights. The re-animates sometimes exhibit behavior to which they have no right; behavior that should belong only to the living.

Blind eyes, with a film of uniform gray, still manage to seem to track you, as if they observe your every movement and catalog it somewhere within the ruins of what was once a mind. The re-animates don't see you, they *can't* see you. And yet they watch you. Heads turn and blind gray sockets fix themselves on you.

You feel those dead eyes on you and it raises the hairs on the back of your neck. And it doesn't matter how hot the day may be, you still feel that cold, primordial chill. You understand how your distant ancestors must have felt as they sheltered in an uncertain world populated by ghosts and monsters and things even worse.

You understand the nature of that fear among those who answered to the names Cro Magnon and Neanderthal. The dread of the supernatural, of something that operated outside all the laws of the living, comes home to you in this present day. In that flash of understanding, that glimpse into history before history, your thoughts drift into dark places, exploring them as if they were caverns opened in the deep stony recesses of an Earth that was far younger than it is now. What might those ancients have known that could chill the spine all these long ages later? What deeply buried memory is it that haunts us?

It is times like that when I wonder if Argus/Jones is something new, or if it is something very, very old. I wonder if, through some accident or odd turn of the season, we managed to reawaken something that had slept since the times when glaciers covered swathes of the globe and buried things that were best left in the ice. Did our distant ancestors know of this plague and somehow survive it? Are there burial sites still hidden from archaeologists, sites where skulls crushed or pierced by flint points might be found? Perhaps, if we survive, we might uncover these remnants someday.

Or perhaps I'm just engaging in idle speculation here.

One thing I know with certainty is that the undead can move with a terrifying speed, given the right circumstances. I have seen this, countless times. The re-animates shamble and shuffle along with that dull motion common to their kind. They move aimlessly, drifting without purpose.

Until they move into the range of the living.

Then they move with the speed of a snake.

The tendons in their neck stretch, their jaws snap and bite, and their motion is nearly swifter than the eye can follow. I have no idea how they can do this, how dead muscles can move with such speed and precision, how a neck can stretch the way it does, and how the jaws can open wide to strike.

But I have witnessed this. I have heard the creak of tendons and the pop of vertebrae, and I have seen motion that is lightning-quick. I have seen them hit with the speed of a cobra, and I have seen them strike the living repeatedly. Sometimes they fall back after a single attack, and sometimes they press things until their victim reels away, mutilated. You can never tell, ahead of time, what shape the attack will take.

All you know is that it will be fast, faster than the dead have any right to move.

But then, the dead should have no right to move at all.

That, I suppose, is the grand paradox right there. These creatures, these tottering hulks, should be dead and in their graves. They should not be shambling among us, and they should not be attacking the living with a speed that belongs more rightly to a pit viper than it does to a corpse.

They should be cold, motionless, and decaying in the places reserved for the dead. They should not be moving. They should not be here.

Yet here they are.

Late August
A Month of Rain

It's raining today. Just as it rained yesterday, and the day before, and the day before that.

And the rains have been soft, and they have been persistent.

And they have been continuing for perhaps a month now.

The world has become sodden. Everything is drenched by the gentle yet relentless fall of the rain, and I cannot help but wonder if Nature has put her hand to scrubbing away the human mark on this planet. I wonder if the rains are only here, or if they are everywhere.

I wonder if Nature is patiently washing the slate clean.

Rainy thoughts fit for rainy days, I suppose.

After the first week of the rains, I found shelter in a small town near what I estimate to be the border of Mississippi and Louisiana. My temporary refuge is a two-story home; a place apparently converted from residence to bed and breakfast hotel. It remains in surprisingly good shape and is a peaceful place to wait out the rainfall. It is infinitely superior to the tent I used for that first week.

The place smells dusty from disuse, but I can find no trace of the decay one expects from the undead or those who fall prey to them. I get the impression that the people who lived here, or took care of this home, left before any of the undead could arrive. Everything was locked tightly and secured against the weather. It is as if everyone was expecting to come back after a short time away.

There is no sign that anyone ever did.

I estimate this house has been abandoned since the outbreak of the plague, almost two years ago.

I'll investigate the rest of the town once the rain subsides, but from here it looks like every place has been locked up like this one. My first view of the town was one of shuttered homes and boarded windows ... everything left in a state of pristine emptiness. It is strange to consider an entire town where the residents chose, in unison, to leave in a single instant and with a single will.

There will be time, later, to learn what became of this town and if any of the living may have chosen some part of it as their last stand against the undead. For now, though, it may be that mine is the only spark of life here ... and that I may be the only being, living or dead, that has set foot in this town since the plague's beginnings.

The thought that there are no predators about, living or undead, should comfort me.

But, in a shuttered home, with windows boarded tight, I sense the weight of ghosts pressing close to me.

The light from my lantern and the glow of the keyboard does nothing to change this feeling. If anything, they make the darkness feel more ominous. They give a sense of depth and substance to the shadows that stir in every corner. It's strange to realize that I feel more comfortable, more secure, outdoors in the rain with only a tent for shelter.

I wonder how well I will sleep tonight.

Or if I will sleep at all.

September
The Abandoned Village

For the past month, I have taken shelter in a home inside an empty town, driven there by rains that simply refused to let up.

I can't recall a time in my life when the rains were so steady or so constant. The strangest part of the whole thing is the fact that the rains were never particularly heavy. They just persisted and never quit. It was as if, for a time at least, the whole world was made of rainy days.

Two days ago, for the first time since I had arrived in this town, the clouds broke. Dry air moved in. Yesterday, I began my exploration of this place.

It is strange to walk these streets, empty yet clean. The town has been abandoned but shows almost no sign of the decay that is all too common elsewhere. These streets seem as if they were swept only a day ago. The shop windows are boarded tight, and the doors are securely locked, but it all feels as though the boards could come down and the doors swing open at a moment's notice.

By every measure of the look, life here could resume without skipping a beat. It would be as though all that has passed was but a momentary disruption, not the upending of the world we knew.

A part of me half-expects to see the shopkeepers return, take down the boards, and scurry back to work. A part of me half expects to see people returning to the streets and homes of this town, picking up their lives and their work exactly where they left off.

I shake my head at the notion. It's all wishful thinking. The cold fact is that nobody is coming back. Those who lived here are long gone. Perhaps they are gone to a place of safety if one exists; perhaps gone and dead.

Or gone, and dead, and walking all the same.

Something icy walks up my neck, even though the day is still warm.

Disturbing thoughts, but they remind me to watch my step. There are things, infinitely patient, that wait in shadows. All they need is for me to forget that, just for a moment.

I spend the week in this town, carefully picking the locks on the doors of various shops or homes that look promising; that look like they may hold stores of non-perishable food or other supplies. It's a long process but rewarding. When I finish my work at each house, and each store, I take care to lock the doors behind me again.

By the end of the week, I've tallied up a virtual treasure trove of goods. I find everything from foodstuffs to clothing and camping supplies. I also find plentiful ammunition, though it's not the sort that I would need. The ammunition consists chiefly of something best suited for a hunter. It's mostly bird- and buckshot. I don't find ammunition for my rifle or my pistol. I take that as a reminder to be sparing with my limited supplies, and to practice more with my bow.

If you're reading this and wondering why I take such care with my inventory, and take even more care to lock up and clean up after myself, the explanation is simple. It's not any attempt to show manners to the empty town. It's a matter of survival in case I ever come this way again. Glass broken from a window frame, or a door that looks forced or is slightly open, can tell me whether a place that was once safe has become dangerous.

Doors and windows which can be locked serve as good barriers against the uninvited, be they undead or still living. More than once, my life has been saved when the sound of something breaking has roused me from sleep.

Looking around this town, I wonder if my habits of caution are all that necessary here. The dust in this place remains undisturbed. Save for some of the smaller wildlife, nothing ... living or dead ... has come this way. Perhaps nothing ever will. But my habits are best left unbroken, even here.

If I ever come back this way, it will be good to know if the town is as safe as it was when I left it.

I am tempted to stay here. Everything I could need for survival and a degree of comfort can be found here; there are even seeds to plant vegetables. The forests outside the town are home to plenty of game. I could do far worse than settling in this place.

But purpose drives me and will accept no change in the bargain I made when I left Florida.

My destination remains the state of Colorado, and Cheyenne Mountain. If I am to find any remnant of civilization, or any attempt to rebuild, I'll find it there.

At least, that's what I keep telling myself.

I'll stay here a little longer. I'll evaluate my supplies to determine what I'll need and will be able to carry.

Then ...

Then, I suppose I'll see what lies beyond this town.

Late September
The Abandoned Village
Reflections on Seasons of Change

A growing sense of the unreal had been tugging at me lately. For some time, it was hard for me to figure out what felt more out of place than usual. After all, I've been walking through a world where the dead no longer stay securely in their graves, sleeping that untroubled dreamless sleep. And, when it comes to the unreal and the unusual, that's about as off the map as it gets.

Then the realization hit me with a flash of the blindingly obvious.

I've been living in this world for almost a year.

I have gone through towns that were either empty or infested with re-animates. I have avoided the undead whenever possible and fought them whenever there was no other choice. I have done battle against those who've used these times as an excuse to shed the last of their humanity.

With rifle and pistol, bow and arrow, I have given the final death to those who should have known rest and peace, but instead knew only the mindless drive to spread a microscopic terror and create more of their kind. I have also turned my weapons against the living, those who would strive to gain the world and make willing sacrifice of their souls. Of the two, I do not know which is worse. I only know that dealing death has become routine.

Everything has changed. Only now, in a place where I would have hoped to find some rest, does the reality of that strike home.

I move through a world that is unrecognizable from the one where I spent my life, and I have come to terms with it. That may be the most unsettling part of it all. Miami, the city I called home for all of my life, has become a stronghold of the undead. The world as I knew it now feels a little more dreamlike every day. And this world, this place where the border of life and death is all but obliterated, feels a little more solid.

A part of my mind reels at the sheer insanity of the prospect. Yet somehow I have come to accept it. The only real surprise is that the world has been this way for almost a year.

I wonder how many more years like this remain?

I sit in twilight, in the dusky room of a boarding house nestled in an abandoned village, and I think of the changes in this world. And it feels perfectly normal to be thinking these thoughts in this place, with no living people to share them.

My calendar is still unreliable, but my date-keeping tells me it has been almost a year. October, an appropriate month, will mark the anniversary of the time when the dead shook off the grave and made this world their own.

How many of the undead move across this world with their shambling mummy feet? How many cities once owned by the living are now populated only by the dead who know nothing of the grave? How many of the living have fallen to this plague?

How many more years like this remain?

And how many of us, if any, will be alive to see them?

September ... Late
The Dream

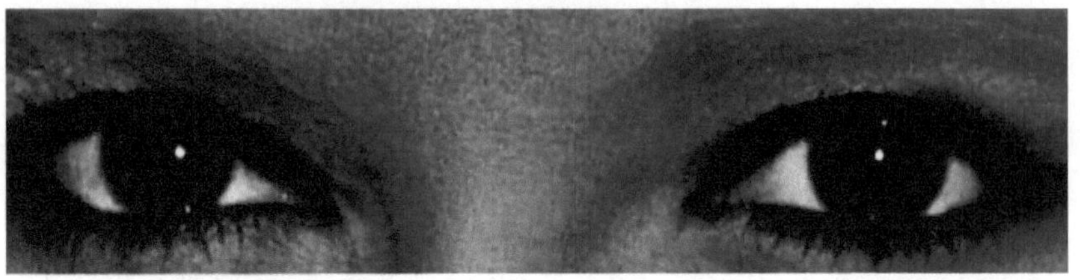

It has been strange to sleep in a real bed, and I confess it took some getting used to. So much of my time has been spent in makeshift camps, tents pitched in deep woods, or a sheltered place. Here, in this abandoned town, things have been different.

Rare have been the nights I have spent in dwellings or other buildings that are not, to some degree or other, a ruin. Rarer still have been the nights spent sleeping on a real bed, with a real mattress and real sheets. It was hard, at first, to get comfortable and know a sound sleep.

This is one of those rarest nights, when my sleep is deep and undisturbed.

That's when she comes to me.

I can't recall the exact moment that she curls up beside me in the bed. All I know is that my sleep has been disturbed by a presence I haven't known for what seems like ages. It feels so natural for her to be there.

I reach out, draw her close to me, feel the silky pressure of breasts against my side, the weight of a hand resting on my chest, the familiar scratch of stiff hairs as she draws a leg over my thigh and snuggles tightly. I had forgotten how much I had missed these sensations.

Her skin is soft yet feels cool and curiously loose. A part of me says I should be alarmed by this, that I should move away from this woman. But that part of me is distant, and its voice is drowned out by the sensations.

A mane of hair tickles me in the hollow of my jaw; soft lips seek out the base of my throat.

There is the delicate bite of teeth breaking my skin, tearing at my flesh.

My blood is hot and thick as it flows from the wound in my neck, gouts of it pumping my life away, moment by moment.

She turns her face to me, her lips and chin reddened with gore against the mummy pallor of her skin. Eyes that are milk-white fix themselves on me as they sag within bony sockets.

Her jagged mouth opens wide.

And I find myself sitting bolt upright, breath rasping in my throat. My heart beats so hard that I can feel the thud of it against my chest, the pounding of blood in my temples. I am literally soaked in my own perspiration.

I reach a tentative hand to my neck and feel only smooth skin. Nothing is torn, and there is no trace of a wound. The bed is clean, with no sign of blood and no impression of any body save my own.

Nothing happened. Nobody was here. It was all a dream, just a dream.

No.

Not a dream.

A nightmare.

I swing my legs over the side of the bed. In the darkness, I feel the carpeted floor solid and substantial under my feet. It's a welcome reminder of the reality of the world. And, with all the horrors of the world, it is still far better than the nightmare I have just escaped.

I have to wonder what it was that triggered this dream. I'd never had anything like it before. Did my sleeping indoors, on a real bed, for so long a time have anything to do with this? Had I let the comfort lull me into a sense of complacency, with my mind sending me this dream as a warning?

Or was it something worse?

I am now acutely aware of the fact that it has been almost a year since the onset of this plague, since the arrival of this disease whose end was terrifyingly worse than death. I have seen few of the living since then, and none I could call companions. And I have no idea how long things will continue to be this way.

I look inside myself and ask the hard questions, the dangerous questions. I look into the shadowed corners of my thoughts, my hand forced by the weight of the nightmare.

After all this time alone, is the isolation finally starting to get to me? Am I so hungry for companionship that I might accept it without regard for my own safety? Is something in my mind finally starting to give?

I shake off that thought, perhaps a bit more forcefully than is necessary. I have moved from introspection to unbridled speculation. No good will come of that. Better to focus on the already difficult job of staying alive without trying to complicate things any further.

But, after this nightmare, I know two things with absolute certainty. First, I'm not going back to sleep tonight. Second, I've stayed in this empty town long enough.

It's time to leave.

Late September
Year Two of the Plague
Back on the Road

I am back on familiar back roads, spending my nights in a tent guarded by a perimeter of trip wires and other alarms, making my way to Louisiana. From there, the roads will take me into Texas and the northern turn toward my eventual destination of Colorado.

It feels strangely good to be traveling again, to be moving with a purpose. I spent what feels like a season in a small, abandoned town, getting far too comfortable for my own good. I had grown accustomed to the town, the place where I had first taken shelter from a month of unrelenting rain. Despite my determination to press ahead with my travels to Colorado, I had let myself get lulled into a complacency and a sense of peace. It took a nightmare to shake me loose.

I've replenished my supplies, charged my batteries, and properly oiled the wheels of my bike. I've also renewed my sense of purpose and left the abandoned town behind. I know the location of the place, and know that I should be able to live out my days there if it comes to that.

But I'm not ready to give that notion more than a passing consideration.

My destination remains Colorado's Cheyenne Mountain, and I am determined to see with my own eyes if civilization has any stronghold there. I will not stop until I have my answer.

The traveling has been easy so far. I have seen no sign of people, either living or undead, and that brings me a sense of relief. I am still able to deal with any trouble I may get into, but I prefer to conserve my dwindling supplies of ammunition. In this area, things are so quiet that a rifle shot will draw the living or the undead from miles around, and I don't want to meet up with either sort.

Strange to realize that I'm no longer comfortable meeting the living. On the one hand, every encounter has the potential to be a confrontation. On the other hand, my discomfort may be keeping me away from scores of potential friends and allies.

Of course, here I am, relishing my solitude and silence even as I make the dedicated effort to seek out a remnant pocket of humanity. And, naturally, I'm sending these words out to the relic corners of the internet for all to see.

That is some industrial-strength cognitive dissonance for you, all right.

I should put out an ad. "Wanted: company for a traveling hermit. Must be relatively non-threatening yet able to hold their own in a fight. Reanimated dead need not apply."

I mentally roll my eyes at the prospect, and it isn't the first time that I've managed to marvel at my ability to hold two wildly contradictory notions at once.

I peddle on, in peaceful silence.

If my maps are correct, the Louisiana border is no more than a day ahead.

Late September
At the Delta

"This far you may come, and no farther..."

I stood at the crumbled edge of an interstate highway, looking at a shoreline leading to the open sea, and all I could think about were those lines from an old religious text.

"This far you may come, and no farther."

The sea in front of me was fog-bound but beautiful; deep blue and tranquil ... filled with the slight brackish tang that is the scent of fresh waters mingling with salt. In every sense, it was the perfect scene of a vast river delta bordering on the open sea.

It was supposed to be the border of Mississippi and Louisiana, and the road ahead to New Orleans.

Now, I suspect that even if I were able to cross this expanse, there would be no city waiting ahead. I have a feeling that New Orleans, and all its history, are gone. Perhaps ruins remain, buried in the sediments and waiting for rediscovery on an uncertain day, or perhaps the sea has scrubbed the city down to its foundations, scattering the remains across the innumerable miles of ocean floor.

What could have created this scene in so short a time? Natural processes could have worn down the coast, but only after ages. This happened maybe inside a year. Something cataclysmic must have happened here.

That's when I remember the month of rain. What was, for me, several weeks of a steady rain, must have been something far worse elsewhere. My rains may well have been the outside limits of a vast storm, something that chewed and hammered at this coast until nothing remained but a greater reach of the Mexican Gulf. It's not the only possibility, but it's one that seems to fit.

Once again, my slow and cautious pace may have saved my life. If I had advanced across the southern gulf states at even a slightly faster pace, the storm that erased this region might have caught me, too.

This far would I have gone. And no farther.

Well. We'll see about that.

I got out my maps and began re-plotting my path.

The plan had been to cross the Gulf into Texas. From there, I had hoped to head north, crossing the Oklahoma Panhandle, and taking a direct route to Colorado.

My eventual destination had been the Cheyenne Mountain Complex. It was my hope that, if any part of a functioning government remained, I would find it there.

Well, that's still the destination. The road might be a bit longer and a bit harder to travel, but that's where I'm going. The only question is how to get from here to there.

I looked through my maps, began plotting my course. There was a way, from Jackson, Mississippi into the southeastern corner of Tennessee. From there, turn west across Arkansas and Oklahoma, then hang a right into Colorado. The last part of the route remains the same. I'll just have to make a few extra turns along a route that may take me longer than I had anticipated.

This was still going to be the most efficient way to get me into Colorado. Hell, who am I kidding? If I want the safest bet, this was probably the only way.

Safe as it may be, relatively speaking, some of this route was going to take me into territory that's rough and more open than I would have liked, but it still looked like my best choice under the circumstances. If something better comes along, I'll take it. For the moment, though, this was the path and that wasn't likely to change.

I tucked my maps away, secured my gear, and turned back the way I had come.

Jackson, Mississippi waited three days ahead of me.

Early October

Year Two of the Plague

Mississippi, along the Road to Tennessee

The Desiccated Man

I made a curious discovery the other day: a sign that there is at least one more living person in this world. More appropriately, a sign that there *was* another living person. Honesty compels me to use the past tense.

What I found was, in fact, a corpse. It was the body of a man, and I have no idea how long he had been dead.

I came across the body as I moved near the shoulder of a back road. I had passed the area of Jackson, Mississippi a few days earlier and was almost at the border of Tennessee. The days had been uneventful, and welcome for all that, until the point when I noticed what appeared to be a body huddled in a heap halfway into the road.

I first saw the corpse as a distant blot on the road. Acting with my customary caution, I moved my bike to the road's edge and parked it, out of sight. I then unshipped my binoculars and settled by the road for a better look. My view revealed the blot to be a body, motionless, sprawled in the middle of the road.

I moved quietly into the underbrush just off the road and settled down, watching the body for any signs of movement. There was no motion, not even the slight rise and fall of the ribcage to indicate breathing. I kept quiet, remaining in the shadows for the better part of the afternoon, making sure that there was no more to the situation than met the eye. Nothing changed. The man remained still and surrounded by silence.

As the shadows of the day stretched toward late afternoon, I decided that I was most likely watching a corpse, and not a carefully set trap. Only then did I put away my binoculars and move. I had kept my movement slow, deliberate, and as silent as possible.

This may sound like excessive caution, but playing things safe has kept me from stumbling into a bad situation more than once. I'm in no hurry to change habits that have kept me alive and mostly out of trouble.

Still exercising care, listening for any stray sounds that could reveal the presence of another person, I moved from my concealment and went to inspect the body. The day remained silent around me. I was alone.

Well, almost alone.

As I had drawn close to the man, I noticed more details about his situation; some clear, some inviting more questions. Most immediately, it became obvious that this man had not been dragged or chased to where he was. He had simply dropped dead in his tracks.

So, what would have caused this? Heart attack, maybe? One thing was sure. I wasn't going to get my answers by standing there and staring at the corpse. I bent to examine the remains.

The man was dressed for travel in rough country, wearing the kind of clothing I would choose for the region. He was wearing a backpack, light but heavy-duty, and full based on the feel of it. Everything showed signs of wear but was well-kept.

The man lay on his stomach, showing no outward sign of trauma. I found no sign of a bullet or knife wound, and no indication of blunt trauma like you'd find with a blow to the skull. The body appeared to be completely intact. Whatever killed this man, it was not some form of violence.

I cut away the pack and turned the body onto its back, continuing my investigation. Tattered remains of hair, plastered to the desiccated skull, appeared brittle and short. The body, curiously light, had skin the consistency of leather. Dried patches against the brown mottled flesh indicated some sort of rash. Almost all the man's teeth were missing.

By this time, I was sweating, hoping that I hadn't stumbled onto a man who had been killed by some new, exotic disease. I started going through his backpack, looking for any kind of clue. Was there medicine? Was there some kind of food that would have spoiled?

I emptied the contents of the backpack onto the road and searched through everything. All I found was a change of clothes and every kind of junk food known to man. No wonder this guy was losing teeth. There wasn't anything remotely healthy in that pack, not even a bottle of vitamins.

And that's when it all came together. I double-checked the mottling of the man's skin and the erosion of his gums, and everything clicked.

Scurvy.

This man had died from scurvy.

I was looking at a man killed by something virtually unknown in an earlier time ... multiple vitamin deficiencies. He couldn't find, or didn't recognize, the right foods to keep him healthy. And he died because of it.

I can only imagine what the poor fellow went through at the end; his uncomprehending suffering. He must have struggled through increasingly hard and painful days, until the day finally came when he fell to the ground and could not get up again. There he lay until the last spark of his life burned out.

Seeing the remains of the man, I found myself thankful for some foresight on my own part. I have kept myself supplied with vitamins, checking pharmacies in every town I visit, and reading about edible plants wherever I go. I have also kept a close watch on the wildlife during the course of my travels. A healthy animal population is a good sign of a healthy food supply.

But, in answering one question, I had dug up another. I knew how this man died, but had no idea when. The body was light and the texture of a mummy, and the collection of dirt and debris around it indicated that the corpse must have lain undisturbed from the moment he fell. I had no idea how long that had been. Weeks? Months?

How long?

The remains were exposed in a temperate area, in the open outdoors, where they should have been prone to an unrelenting attack from microbes and the elements. The body should have begun decomposing immediately. There should have been nothing left for me to inspect.

Yet there was no trace of decay or decomposition in the corpse. While something was happening to the body, it looked more like weathering ... or erosion. The man's remains were damn near pristine, and they might stay that way for years for all I could tell.

So, what has happened?

What has happened to the microscopic universe that has governed the cycle of life, death, and decomposition? Has nature declared some strange truce in the face of this overwhelming plague, letting other forms of illness and harm stand aside at least for a time?

Or has the virus that brings the living death brought a change to all scales of being, and not just creatures as biologically complex as humans? I have no answers, only some damned unsettling questions.

But it would be supremely ironic if the virus that turns the living into the reanimated dead is also the great cure for every other disease that has plagued humanity from its beginnings.

October
Year Two of the Plague
Near the Mississippi Border
The Scent of Halloween

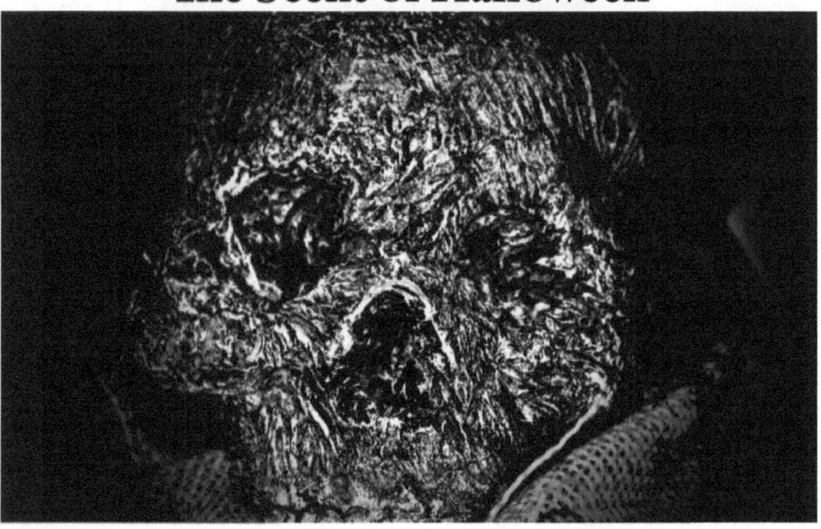

I believe we are nearing the season of Halloween, though my computer calendar remains unreliable in that regard. It still can't track the dates consistently, and I've given up trying to fix that function. I've been sticking with my admittedly low tech approach to date-keeping. That is, I've been marking off the days on my laptop's notepad and any scratch paper I can find.

The weather has the distinct feel of fall about it. Leaves are changing color in a way I have never seen firsthand, and there is a surprisingly refreshing bite to the air. I'm not leaning on instinct when I estimate that the month is October. There's the evidence of nature to back me up. Well, nature and my ersatz calendar.

This is autumn, and probably the first or second week of October. I'll admit that my date-keeping is off by a week or two, but it's no more than that. I've always been good at having an instinctive handle on time.

That means this is the anniversary of the outbreak. That's the thing that floors me. I find it so hard to believe that a little more than a year has passed since the outbreak of this plague. It's difficult to parse the passage of time, given the utter change brought so swiftly by this infernal disease.

Before this time, I would have looked at the passage of days as a time when small things might change but where more would just stay the same.

Now, it seems as if there is the barrier of a life, a world, an entire universe between me and those days.

Irony, in its purest shape, marks this time of year.

It was with the approach of the season of the dead that the virus began its march across the populated world.

Chalk paper skeletons crumbled, gave their ground to something darker and more relentless.

The clatter of bone faded in the leather shuffle of feet long dead ... but feet that never knew the grave.

Late was the hour then, and now so much later still.

I write this by the light of a campfire, waiting to transcribe these words into the journal I began keeping an age ago.

Electricity still lives, but it's a more furtive thing. Power is now best conserved, husbanded and guarded with a fine jealousy.

And the candles and torches, the fires lit against the dark, are perhaps better companions for these times, when life is as uncertain as the flow of current, and breath can be snuffed by a vagrant breeze.

The leaves turn their colors in the northern reaches of this continent. Red and gold tumble to the ground and bring a fine carpet.

But there is no smell of woodsmoke, no tang of pumpkin, and no candy or laugh of make-believe goblins for still another year.

It saddens me to think that the change of autumn's colors are seen through few human eyes, that most of the eyes that witness the seasons are dull gray and uncomprehending. There is nothing of life in those eyes to marvel at the season; to ponder the change in color or the scent of approaching winter.

As a world prepares for sleep, it may be that a mere handful of the living are left to see the change of seasons.

And so pure is the irony now. A second Halloween approaches and there are no ghosts.

Just the dead ... and the graves they abandoned long ago.

Mid-October
The Road to Tennessee
and Reflections on a Late Night

Another night on the road, and I write these notes with my camp bathed in moonlight.

A part of me regards the cascade of silver light as a helpful thing. Should something unwelcome attempt to encroach on my camp site, I'll have substantial visual warning of it.

A clear line of sight, however, isn't my only ally on nights like this. I take other precautions, such as still ringing my camp with trip wires and noisemakers. Whether the night is brightly lit or dark with only the scattering of stars, I still must sleep sometime. My perimeter alarms give me comfort, and the certainty of a decent amount of warning. Time enough to be alert and ready, no matter how sound the sleep.

But there is more to this than the need for sleep and security. The night brings a certain clarity with it, a chance for reflection, and even the rare moment of hope. It is the kind of hope that becomes evident only when the sun sets, and the stars come out.

With electricity all but relegated to myth, there is still evidence that we once commanded a magnificent technology. I know this, for I have seen it.

In the moonless nights, I have seen the coursing of satellites as they whisper their way across the face of the dark, like so many hurried stars. These are not the distant weather satellites that keep pace with the rotation of the Earth. These are the low-flying satellites of the Night Telegraph system; a web of orbiting technological marvels that once bound the world together through voice and data. The system, itself, was the brainchild of a man who was part Hollywood innovator, part rebel inventor, part madman, and part legend. Regardless of what may have come of this man, his invention still lives.

Perhaps these words, written by turns in a tent or in a makeshift shelter and uploaded to uncertain currents, are gathered up like so many electromagnetic threads and woven into the digital speech of these satellites; engraved in the high arcane language of a technology only the machines may know, at least for the time being. I wonder if it's possible that the words I write have been carefully stored by these orbital caretakers, husbanded against a day when some may again find the tools to read them.

For all I know, the Night Telegraph is where these words will live once I've sent them from my computer. It is possible that the machines will be the final caretakers of these human words. The satellites of the Night Telegraph may tell and re-tell these stories across the arc of years, whispering them as their human progenitors once whispered tales born of the deep legends.

But I have seen a thing that gives me pause to hope. I have seen the space station. It moves as a larger star, rising in the west and setting in the east, reminiscent in my thoughts of the old sailing ships that would make regular transit from one horizon to another.

The space station was the creation of the same mad genius who built the Night Telegraph system, but it was something even more special than the Night Telegraph. It was designed as an amalgam of research outpost, tourist get-away, and way station for those pioneers who worked at Luna Base, the research facility located on the near side of the moon in the aptly named Sea of Crises. It was the one reliable link of the living from this world to those whose footprints mark the lunar surface.

I wonder what may have become of the scientists at that most far-flung enclave of humanity. Did they fall to the same virus as the people of this world? Did they die the slow death of those who were faced with dwindling resources as the freight ships no longer rose from Earth, but lay rusting in their launch cradles?

Or did they survive?

Did the scientists of that distant base defy the odds and carve out their own survival from the unforgiving lunar rock? Did they manage the impossible, even as any chance for help withered a quarter million miles away? Do they, even now, look through their telescopes toward Earth? Residents of one dead world regarding another?

We may never know. All contact with the base was lost early in the plague. It happened at around the same time we lost touch with the space station. All ground-based communication fell silent as bases were either abandoned by the living or overrun by the undead. The answers, if there are any to be had, must wait for a day when we may yet struggle to reclaim the sky, and the night above the Earth.

And what of the space station, and the man who designed it? What became of him?

There are those who say the mad inventor rode the last ship up from Earth, refusing to leave his creation alone and unattended, and determined to keep it from drifting and eventually tumbling back to Earth in the fires of a catastrophic re-entry. Looking at the constant star making its nightly rounds, It is easy to believe the inventor found a way.

Perhaps he is still there, on board his space station. Perhaps he is keeping an old Earthly tradition, standing the last watch, and holding lonely vigil in an unending night.

Or perhaps he failed in his efforts. Perhaps the inventor of legend found nothing but his own end above the Earth and is now numbered among those long dead.

It may be the star I watch at night is not a beacon of hope, but a ghost ship, with a spectral captain at the helm.

Late October or Early November
Year Two of the Plague
Outside Memphis

I have been feeling a chill in the air, which tells me autumn is waning and the year is moving toward winter. As the cooler air descends, I am finding myself farther north than I had expected to be.

New Orleans had been my intended destination for this season, but that was before the storm that brought the creation of an inland sea at what was once the Mississippi line. Louisiana, for all I know, remains under waters that may stretch into southeastern Texas. The discovery was a shock that forced a change in my travels. I was compelled to backtrack, then move up through Mississippi and into lower Tennessee. My destination remains Colorado, but I am taking the long way.

Now the bite in the air, though an unfamiliar thing to me, rings as a signal bell that the seasons have begun their change and cold weather encroaches. I need to start looking for a place where I can shelter for the winter. Biting cold and the potential for snow are new things to someone who has spent his life in the subtropical climate of Miami and, to a lesser degree, the warmth of the lower Gulf states.

I know very little of winter, so I plan to take it seriously. The world in which I walk is one where mistakes and miscalculations can carry a death sentence. I don't intend to be taken by surprise in the event of unexpected cold or a random snowfall.

I've already taken out my maps and studied the routes ahead. I've been looking for areas where the roads are well-marked, if not well-traveled, where small out-of-the-way towns might be found.

The goal is to find a place which has necessities within reach, but which also is sheltered from the re-animated dead and the predatory living. A small town in a wooded area, or nestled in foothills, would be ideal for my purposes.

Fortunately for me, I still have a little time to study the roads and topography ahead and select the best path to take. I've got two weeks, maybe a month, before I have to stop my travels and settle in for the winter. By then, I should have reached the destination of my choice and be settled.

If all goes well, I'll have found a place to stay long before the cold becomes a problem. I might even have some spare time to move on if my first choice doesn't work out. If there are too many re-animates, then I'll still be able to find another place to stay that is out of their reach.

The undead have been rare things of late; the living have been rarer still.

There is time enough to plan the routes and make my choices for the winter.

For now, my thoughts turn to Memphis, two days behind me in my journey.

I have walked through a city of some legend and find myself haunted by it; the words of a singer echoing within the chambers of my memory, asking if W.C. Handy would look down over me. I wonder if that person resides in Memphis as a benevolent ghost, protecting those like myself, travelers who are just walking through the city toward an uncertain destination. It's a comforting thought for me in a melancholy time.

Tennessee is a place where there is no shortage of legends, where people stand astride the border of humanity and myth. Some of those people are the stuff of early folk tales, others have grown as legends only in later years.

I remember one singer, a man who achieved that stature. He was, as I remember, a complex man whose talent was nearly overshadowed by certain excesses. Some say he was cut down by a heart attack when he was barely into middle age. Others wove webs of "what-ifs," speculating that the man had grown tired of the pressures of the spotlight and had vanished to a peaceful retirement under the mantle of an assumed death. I find myself half-wishing that the more outlandish of the stories might be true, and that the singer may yet live and be planning a campaign to re-take his home state.

Then, my thoughts turn to another vocalist. If Tennessee has patron angels, she must surely be among them. There is no rumor about her, no speculation. Before the fall of Miami, she had been alive and in full vigor. She might be living still. I hope that's the case. I imagine her as an angel with blonde tresses and the sharp-shooting skills of a latter-day Annie Oakley. There is solace in the thought of this vocalist leading a charge against the re-animates, raising morale as she smiles a ready smile and takes a deadly aim on the undead who cross her sights. She was an impressive person before the advent of the plague. Who knows but she may have become truly formidable now.

I imagine it's possible that these vocalists, and others, may still stand guard in the cities and mountains of Tennessee. I haven't seen anyone, but that's of little consequence. Memphis is big and can accommodate living fighters as well as kindly ghosts or patron saints. In a city this size, I could pass by any of those and never notice. The city is as large as legend.

I leave Memphis behind, a city of fable that shares its name with another city of ancient renown. May the Memphis of Tennessee become as legendary as the Memphis of Egypt.

November
Year Two of the Plague
Halfway through Arkansas
The Zealots

I have learned a new skill: cold-blooded murder.

And may God damn the people who taught me.

Let's be clear. I've killed before and done so more than once. Whether it was the undead, the insane, or the living predatory human, I've used the tools at my disposal to stop the re-animates or to end lives outright. I chose my life over the lives of those who would do me harm.

I didn't always like it, and there was a part of my mind that nagged at me over whether killing was the best course to take. It would demand that I examine whether I had killed only after exhausting all other options ... or whether my imagination and intellect had failed and had let me trap myself into that one course of action.

Even in killing the undead there was a sense of regret. The re-animates had stopped their decay at some point, and now moved like leathery husks stretched over bone and paper-thin mummy flesh. But still I wondered if they were well on their way to that final death ... that end which comes to us all.

Not this time; no way. What I did was murder. Pure and simple and with blood the temperature of ice water.

It began when I heard voices near a farmstead.

I was somewhere near the middle of Arkansas, if what I had learned from my maps still held true. I was traveling my back roads on my bicycle, moving at a pace that was slow, sedate, and so very quiet; just as I liked it. I was in no hurry and was making no noise.

I heard the voices long before they could have been aware of me, and I was able to dismount my bike and hide it in some brush at the roadside. It would be invisible to a casual inspection, and there were none who would be of a mind for a detailed examination of the overgrowth.

I was in the perfect position to observe these people, and determine their motives, without them being the least bit aware of me. That was exactly how I wanted it. Experience had taught me the value of silence, and it was a lesson I had no intention of forgetting.

Creeping up on the voices, keeping as still and silent as the shadows that concealed me, I came across a thing that may haunt me for as long as I remain on this Earth.

The voices came from what I can only describe as a religious gathering of some twisted sort. I couldn't tell exactly what it was, but it belonged to no religion I had ever known. And if a hell exists, I was looking down the throat of it.

People dressed in tattered linen vestments, eyes glassy and wide, arms uplifted to something unknowable, were chanting in a strange plain song as a ragged line of the undead marched toward them from the far side of an open field.

Between the undead and the singers, huddled in the middle of the field, was a group of small children ... frightened and dressed in the whitest white.

As the re-animates approached, I saw the children apparently struggling to get up and escape ... but something held them back. I unshipped my binoculars for a closer look. I saw ropes, with knots expertly tied.

The children had been tethered to stakes, left in the middle of the field as an offering.

There was nothing I could do to save them.

That may have been the most wrenching, stomach-churning fact with which I had to come to terms. I was armed, but not well enough to deal with both the re-animates and those who summoned them.

And I was sickeningly, pathetically out of time ... for as soon as I realized the scope of the thing happening in the field outside, the undead were already on top of the children.

And unearthly moaning combined with unholy plain song and the cries and shrieking of children ... cries cut mercifully short.

I turned my head from the scene, unable to watch as the tiny, white robes became stained crimson ... as the most vulnerable of people fell to the most mindless brutality.

After a time, things fell silent. The zealots stayed quiet and still while the re-animates milled about. Soon, with no sound or motion on the part of those who yet lived, the undead started shambling away, an aimless wandering with no clear destination.

The zealots, in single file, began walking in a different direction. I followed them, quietly and at a distance. An ugly idea was already taking shape.

I tracked them to a barn-like structure not too distant from the open field and watched them file inside, closing a heavy door behind them.

Using my binoculars, I examined the structure, keeping to the shadows the whole time. I found only one door and no ground level windows that weren't solidly boarded up.

Good.

I melted back into the shadows and made my way back to the road. I spent the rest of the day siphoning what gasoline I could from the tanks of wrecked cars, pouring it into a salvaged gas can from another of the vehicles. There wasn't much uncontaminated gasoline to be found, but I wasn't going to need much for my purposes.

As the shadows lengthened and the day headed toward evening, I made my way back to the barn. I carefully poured the gasoline around the perimeter of the structure.

I knew the smells of cooking and unwashed bodies inside would mask any stray fumes.

There was pine straw on the ground, and I knew it was dry enough to hold the gasoline, but not let it evaporate.

When I had finished, I took a flare from my pockets, pushed it into the ground, and struck it to life with the friction cap.

From there, I moved into the woods directly across from the door of the barn, settled into deep cover, and waited.

Night and full darkness had arrived by the time the flare burned down to the gasoline-soaked pine straw. The fire started and caught almost instantly. In less than a handful of minutes, the flames had encircled the structure and were chewing their way into it.

Prone on the ground, my rifle propped steadily, I sighted on the front door and waited.

Inside, people had begun to smell smoke and feel the touch of heat. The front door flung open, revealing a figure dark against the firelight.

I aimed my weapon and squeezed the trigger.

The impact of the bullet made the figure tumble back inside the barn.

Four times more a figure appeared in the firelight. And four times more I sent them tumbling back inside the structure.

I fired slowly, methodically, with all the calculation and all the emotion of a machine.

I heard voices, raised and imploring, though the fire garbled the words. That was fine with me.

They called out, and I answered with deliberate rifle shots.

After a time, the only sound was the fire.

By dawn, the structure had burned to embers.

I got up from my sniper's nest and walked around the remains of the building. Nothing in the ashes moved, and no footprints led away from the place. The scorched remains of a concrete slab told me that it was unlikely this place had a cellar of any sort. It was with an ugly satisfaction that I surveyed the charred skeletons scattered in the smoking ruins. Nothing had escaped. Everything that had been inside this place was dead, and it would harm no one again.

I left the smoldering remains of the barn and went to the field where the children had died.

I dug graves for them and, as tenderly as I could, I laid the bodies inside and covered them in the sheltering earth.

Recovering my bike and my gear, I spent the day leaving that damnable place far behind me.

I was out of ammunition for my rifle, so I flung the thing into the first pond I found. The weapon was useless to me, but I didn't want anyone else to find and try to use it.

That night, in the outskirts of an abandoned city, I slept and dreamed that the children came to me.

Taking their hands, I led them to a place of sailing ships and clean waters.

November
Year Two of the Plague
More Thoughts Attend an Anniversary

More than a year has passed since the onset of the undead and the time Argus/Jones became an everyday part of our vocabulary. The time of late September into early October marked that anniversary, and I still find myself dwelling on it from time to time. I know that there's nothing to be gained by looking toward a past that no human agency can change, but I've still seen my thoughts wandering in that direction.

I don't blame myself for letting my thoughts sift through the accumulation of days, weeks, and months. Some anniversaries pack more impact than others. And, if there is an anniversary that punches harder than this one, I don't know what it could be.

A sense of melancholy and loss has come with my recollection of that time and the cataclysmic nature of the change that came with it. Maybe my encounter with the zealots and the children I failed to save turned my thoughts down this darker path. Maybe it was that nightmare I've not been able to shake since it first haunted me in a town besieged by a month of rain. Maybe it was the early realization that I had waged a solitary war against the re-animates for almost a year.

Hell, maybe it's just the fact that the days are growing darker earlier with the change of seasons. I can't say for certain what has caused these thoughts, but I've been working to sort through them, cope with them, and file them away in their proper places in memory. Lord, it has been a draining thing.

It's times like these that I'm glad I never got close to anyone else after my divorce. I've been worried enough about my ex-wife and her family. God only knows how I'd be feeling, or what might have happened, if I'd formed closer ties to another person. My memories are torment enough as it is.

The last time I spoke with my ex-wife was October a year ago. I'd let her know that I had spent the sum of three alimony payments in gathering supplies for what might be an extended camp-out as the plague gathered steam. She had been surprisingly understanding, and had confided fears of her own. She was living in Ohio with her family, not far from the Canadian border, and they had been watching news reports about how the border was getting fortified. People were being checked and strip-searched for any signs of bites. She'd been clear that she was worried about that but was perfectly willing to accept the intrusion if it meant getting to a safe place, a place where the dead stayed dead. Reflecting on that conversation, I have found myself hoping that she and her family were able to reach that safe place. I may never know for sure, but I'll cling to that hope.

I've also found myself thinking about other stories from the early days of the plague. There had been scattered news reports of entire families being killed by a loved one who had kept silent about being infected. There had been other stories of families who had chosen to die together in a mass suicide rather than face an end that was worse than the grave. I've wondered if I might have fallen into one of those groups if things had been different, if I'd been more comfortable with taking a chance on getting close to people again.

Ironically, solitude was easier for me when there were more of the living around. Friendships were casual to the point of being expendable. I could hang out with some of my co-workers and never have to wonder how I might feel if I never saw those people again. Sometimes, a co-worker would find another job or another life somewhere else, and it might be months before the rest of us would realize someone was missing from the group. It is strange to look back on those days when the living were so plentiful that people like me could take refuge in this kind of anonymity. I could drift from one day to the next and never have to worry about the loss of someone close, because there was never anyone who fit that description. There was only the sea of the casual and the faceless.

Now I'm among what may be the few who remain alive. There are no more living crowds where I can lose myself. I am moving with a purpose, but I am moving on my own. I'm paying for this in the coin of loneliness, and it can sting. But I made my choice long ago, when I chose to steer clear of close relationships. I'm not going to whine about a decision I made with my eyes wide open.

It can hurt to live with this decision, and dreams can haunt me from time to time. But that's the price, and I agreed to pay it. Maybe there's a lesson in humanity here, waiting for me at Cheyenne Mountain. Maybe I'll be able to learn from this.

All I have to do is stay alive long enough to find out.

November
Arkansas, Near the Oklahoma Border
On Foot

I have become a hiker.

My trusty bike broke down just before I reached the Oklahoma border, and there wasn't a bloody thing I could do to fix it. I've had the bike break down on me before, and I've always been able to tinker up a repair of some sort, but the accumulation of miles and bad roads conspired to snap about a half dozen spokes on both tires, putting my front and rear wheels completely out of round. As a final insult, my chain snapped in two places with little metal bits flying into the overgrown brush roadside.

It would have taken an incredible amount of luck and skill to repair my bike, and I was pretty sure I didn't have enough of either one.

So, that was game over for my trusty aluminum steed. I dropped the kickstand, parked my bike in one final place, and strapped on my pack and supplies.

From there, I started walking.

It was going to be a long way to Colorado on foot, but at least I had covered this much ground before becoming a pedestrian. And there was always the chance that I would come across a hardware store which hadn't been completely pillaged. Maybe I'd find another bike before much longer.

Either way, I thanked providence for the foresight to build a wheeled travois, pack sensibly, and even exercise enough so that I could cover ground without wiping myself out. If I had faced these circumstances when I first left Miami, I probably would have called it quits and walked into the ocean.

Oklahoma

Reflections on a Hot Shower

I'm in a reflective mood today. I find myself thinking about some of the luxuries we have, which are things we never used to give a second thought. I doubt we ever took anything so for granted as we did our technology ... and the older the tech, the less we noticed it.

I was somewhere in the middle of Oklahoma, and not all that far from the Colorado state line, when I got reacquainted with one of the simplest of luxuries ... a warm-water shower.

It was a day after a raid on a small camping store. I'd gone in there looking for a replacement for my bike, but without any luck. Oh, I had found a couple of bicycles, but both of them had tires rotted beyond use. I turned the store upside down looking for spares or inner tubes, but didn't find a thing.

I did, however, find one of those "disposable" kits for a camp shower. An easy principle: fill the bag with water, hang it in direct sunlight, and let Sol do the rest.

The bag looked like one of the ever-present artifacts of our earlier age: durable, yet still disposable with no great hardship incurred. Not anymore, those days were gone.

I did as the bag instructed and spent my day checking my supplies. What did I need? What did I have? What had been used beyond my capacity to repair? The serviceable items were carefully repacked, the worn-out items were carefully buried, and the soil made to look undisturbed.

From my earliest days on the road I'd felt it was best to leave as few clues to my campsites as possible. I had left caches in the cities

I had passed through, but they were deliberate and designed to be found. I was a bit more circumspect with my own footprints.

You can call it paranoia if you like, but I just felt safer keeping my profile as low as possible. There had been a handful of occasions when my profile was not as low as it should have been and I had ended up drawing unwelcome attention. The bandits who thought this made me an easy mark had learned otherwise. That education put them all in graves, so they're damned unlikely to discuss my movements with anyone.

Work done, I returned to the moment. The splash of warm water brought back that familiar flood of memories, of a time when there was electricity and air-conditioning; of the smell of soap and the crisp feel of freshly washed clothes ... or a hot meal cooked and eaten while watching or ignoring whatever was on Television.

Of a time when the line of demarcation between life and death was definite and clear.

Strange to walk in one world, but carry the memories of another, of a world that may be as far out of reach as Ancient Rome. Sometimes I find myself dwelling in that world and remembering it as being better than it was.

I let my camp shower dry out, then packed and stowed it, still musing about the change in attitudes; even now, even with me.

I've grown used to bathing in cold streams, using sand instead of soap, and trapping more of my food as a matter of routine.

The idea of a hot shower feels like luxury.

And it gets me to thinking about something else.

I wonder if there is still coffee anywhere.

It might be worth my time to scout around for some, and a pot to brew it.

Hot coffee. Lord, but there is a luxury for sure.

November
Oklahoma
Practice with Bow and Arrows

It was once said that the bow and arrow were invented by someone who wanted to stab someone else ... but from a safe distance.

I'm pretty sure that was never true, but I admire the attitude behind the saying. Keep your friends close, and your enemies as far away as possible.

The archaeologists of our past would probably figure that the bow and arrow most likely came from ideas pieced together by the hunter/gatherers of pre-history. Mind you, the people of that time were hunting game that had them outclassed by probably a thousand pounds or so; game that came complete with claws and sharp teeth or antlers and a bad attitude.

I'm willing to bet that the hunters of bygone days preferred to launch an arrow at these targets rather than risk getting inside their personal space.

So, I've taken the hint from my long-removed forbears, and I have taken every chance to practice with the bow.

The bow was my first choice as a weapon against the re-animates; a decision made after long consideration, even when I had my rifle. So far, the choice has proved to be a good one. The investment of effort in my practicing has been solid.

And I have become deadly with this instrument.

I won't lie. My skill came only after tireless research and practice, and only after several early mistakes and dead ends. My first choices in bows and arrows were terrible. Had I stayed with them, they would have killed me by now. Thankfully, I was able to learn from my early mistakes, and correct them.

I now have a stubby compound bow and an arsenal of heavy composite arrows. I have practiced whenever opportunity can afford it, until use of the weapon has become effortless and second nature.

A compound bow may not seem like the best choice of weapon against the undead. It is relatively close range when compared to other projectile weapons, and it is not an easy thing to master. I have found, however, that the advantages outweigh the drawbacks. Most practical among the advantages is the fact that the ammunition is reusable. A bullet, once fired, is gone for good. An arrow can be recovered and used again, sometimes several times.

There are other considerations, as well. Bullets, in sufficient quantity, are heavy. Every pound you carry in ammunition is a pound you can't carry in basic supplies. If I have ten pounds of bullets, then that's ten pounds I can't use for anything else. Food, water, first-aid gear ... something has to be sacrificed so that I can carry the ammunition I need.

The same goes for rifles. There are weight and storage considerations for them, and they need to be cleaned religiously. So, let's add the weight and mass of gun oil and cleaning supplies to our inventory of bullets. When every ounce has to be carefully weighed and considered, you start to see rifles and ammunition in a different light.

Ammunition is also impermanent. Nobody is making it anymore. Oh, you may be able to find some in an area that has not been raided or looted, but the odds of finding the right caliber of ammunition were not that good to begin with; and they have grown vanishingly small ever since. With no bullets, a rifle stops being a long-range weapon and becomes a club.

That's what happened with me. I had carried a military rifle and ammunition, thanks to the last act of a soldier now long dead, and the weapon had served me well. It kept me alive while I learned how to use the bow and arrow, and it served me through some dark times and darker necessities. But the day came when the firing pin struck with an empty click. I chucked the weapon into a pond, letting it sink to the bottom where no one would ever find it.

I still carry a pistol and about twenty rounds of ammunition, along with a few sticks of dynamite found in an abandoned construction site, but I am under no illusions. Those are last-chance weapons. If I am forced to use them, then it's a good bet that I'll be in the sort of bind that nobody escapes alive. Oh, I'll fight tooth and nail, that's what last chances are for. Win or lose, and it'll probably be "lose," I'll make a lot of noise.

That brings me to the biggest reason why I have chosen the bow. Guns, no matter what steps you take, make noise. And that noise will attract any re-animates that happen to be nearby. The undead react to sound, and they home in on its source. The bow, on the other hand, is as silent as a whisper. It kills quietly.

I have learned to keep the distance where the muffled twang of a bowstring goes unnoticed by the undead, even as they fall to my arrows. I have moved with a lethal silence and killed re-animates without them ever being aware that the final death was among them.

As I noted earlier, I have become deadly with this instrument.

And it's a good thing that I've learned to use the bow as well as I have. I suspect I'll have need of my skills before much longer.

I have noticed, in recent days, that small game has gone missing from the traps I have set for it. It doesn't happen everywhere I set my traps, but it's obvious that food is being stolen, and the thing that steals it is not leaving any trace. And it has been happening every place I go.

So I practice with my bow, because I may need to use all the skills I have ... and I may need to use them soon.

Because I believe something is hunting me.

Oklahoma, Northwest of Enid
My Hunter Revealed

I find myself dealing with an unexpected revelation, and to be honest, some unexpected feelings. I believe things may have changed for me now, as profoundly as they changed for all of us when this plague first surfaced. This change, though, is ... well ... different.

On the one hand, I now walk through a world where the undead outnumber the living; where caution is the key to survival and where even some of the living can be more dangerous than the dead. On the other hand, I have acquired an amiable stalker, maybe a friend.

I suppose an explanation is in order.

It all began when I noticed that small game had gone missing from traps I had set.

It was, and remains, a common practice for me to set traps if I am to stay in a particular place for a day or two. In the right season, I can catch squirrel and rabbit, and that sets the table well enough in times when other food is scarce. If the traps are vacant, that means a night with an empty stomach. Mind you, I've learned how to go a few days without having anything to eat. I have been through periods where I was lucky to get maybe three meals in a week. But that doesn't mean I have to like it.

And when something is robbing my traps, I have to wonder what its plans may be. I have to ask if I am being hunted by something ... and I have to ask what I may need to do about it.

Today, as fall gives way to a proper winter, all my questions have been answered and the nature of the hunter revealed. And the stubborn fact is, as prepared as I thought myself to be for anything,

I   was   not   prepared   for   what   I   found.

My hunter is whiskered, covered in fur, and weighs somewhere in the neighborhood of twenty or twenty-five pounds.

I was cooking a rabbit I had caught, letting it spit-roast over my fire, when he walked into my campsite just as bold as brass — a rangy adult cat, long legged and lanky, absolutely feral and absolutely unafraid of me. He looked at the cooking rabbit, looked at me, then looked back at the rabbit. Then he sat down by the campfire, just across from me.

Perched. And sat.

And nothing more.

It was in that moment I knew I was looking at the culprit who had been robbing my traps systematically. He must have been following me ever since I left Memphis, waiting and snatching meals from the traps I had set, never leaving a trace of his actions. Somehow, he had managed to take the occasional squirrel or rabbit and leave no evidence other than an empty sprung trap.

And now, for a reason I could not comprehend, this feral creature had chosen to walk into my campsite and make himself known to me in the most staggeringly bold fashion. Had he grown tired of taking food from my traps and chosen to let me do all the work now? Had he decided that cooked food might taste better, and he wanted to try some?

Had he decided he no longer wanted to walk alone?

Whatever his reasons, this cat had chosen to enter my space and claim a portion of it for himself. As is the way with all cats, he had not bothered to ask for my opinion. As I watched, he continued to sit there, tail curled around his feet, waiting for the rabbit to finish cooking.

I looked at this small intruder and quirked up an eyebrow.

"Well, hello there, little fellow."

The cat looked at me and favored me with a slow blink, but otherwise didn't move.

Of the two of us, I believe I was the more startled by my speaking. My voice, while soft and paper thin, sounded strange ... almost alien to me. And I realized that I hadn't spoken in maybe a year or more, not since the outbreak of the plague. My voice sounded so out of place because I had not used it. There had been nothing, all this time, but my thoughts. Now, I had company.

I pondered this while the rabbit finished cooking. My guest seemed to be content to leave me to my thoughts, at least until the rabbit was done. Once the cooking was finished, he stirred himself.

"Not now, little fellow. We need to let this cool." I stuck the spit into the ground beside me, rabbit-side up, and let the heat vent from it.

The cat seemed to consider my words for a moment. Then he sat back down, this time a little closer to me. Again, he looked at me with a long feline patience. That look seemed to tell me that he had given matters a great deal of thought and had decided that I might ... in time ... be a somewhat decent choice of company.

After a while, the rabbit had cooled to the point where it was warm enough to eat, but not blisteringly hot. I tore a haunch from it and set it down in the grass beside me. The cat promptly got up, walked over, and settled down to his dinner.

I sat there, watching the little guy who had been crafty enough first to steal from me, then bold enough to introduce himself to me. He had been a clever little rascal, clever as a ...

I reached over and scratched him behind one of his ears.

"...Why you little Fox. Hello."

He looked up briefly, then went back to eating. But he was purring.

It took me a long time to realize I was smiling.

Oklahoma
The Border
The Undead

There's a thing about the undead.

They don't always moan.

That was something I learned a long time ago when I first encountered them.

They shuffle along, moving with an unsettling aimless purpose, their clouded eyes fixed on some distant goal or object that only they can see, and they stay utterly silent.

Until they notice you.

Then their heads turn, and those sightless eyes fix themselves on you ... bore into you.

Then mouths open, jaws creak on leather hinges, and the moaning begins.

The dead shuffle toward you, as silent and certain as the erosion of life itself, and they make that low wailing utterance; a whistling of air passing over long dead vocal cords in an unearthly dirge.

If there is only one re-animate, its moans will attract others and draw them to you. If there is a group of the undead, then each will take up the moan one after the other until you are all but deafened or driven mad by a paralyzing fear. And there is always, always that steady approach as they advance on you, walking on dead feet and the scent of the grave.

There are times when the moaning is a faint, reedy whistle coming from deep in the throat, a piping that sounds somehow mournful in its quality. You hear that, and you almost feel sorry for the creatures. You get the sense that they are lamenting a life that is left in tatters, where only vagrant memories lurk in distant corners of a ruined brain. You wonder if they are sobbing through throats of mummified flesh and weeping from eyes long dry of tears.

Then they turn on you and begin that steady tread toward you; and you realize the sorrow is as much a counterfeit of life as the shambling gait of the undead. You understand that all sense of self and all sense of life are long gone. If graves exist in this world, then you might find those remnants of life and self buried deep within them, in the places where these bodies should rightfully be interred.

Of the creatures in front of you, no shred of humanity remains.

And you run. You run as if your life depends on it, because it does. You run to outrace the sound and you run to escape the dead who move as deliberately as a nightmare. And you run for the entire day if that's what it takes to hear nothing but silence behind you.

I know. I have done this.

Fox and I were near the Oklahoma border when we were caught off guard.

We were walking through a ruined suburb, an anonymous collection of houses that all looked alike and, in an earlier life, would have been under the benign tyranny of a homeowners' association. I had hoped there might be something worth salvaging here, but my hopes were turning sour. The neighborhood looked abandoned. Some homes had a ransacked look; others had been damaged by fire. It all looked completely empty.

I never heard the sound of gravel dislodged by a footstep, but Fox did.

My companion's ear twitched and swiveled, his head snapped left, his back arched, and his mouth opened in a low growling hiss.

I followed his gaze, and I saw the nightmare pouring out of the ruined homes. There were dozens of them coming with that slow and relentless tread — all of them moving in utter silence.

There was no way I could kill all of them, even if I made all of my arrows count. Fox and I were hopelessly outnumbered.

And the re-animates hadn't made a sound.

I grabbed Fox up in my arms, and I ran.

I ran until the only sound was the blood pounding in my ears, until my vision got blotchy and shot through with stars, until my breath was a tearing burn in my throat and every heartbeat was a pulsing agony in my chest.

Then I ran farther still. And I stayed silent, as desperately silent as I could, terrified that even my breath could give me away.

After what felt like miles, I lost my footing, stumbled to a halt, and fell to my knees. I spilled Fox out of my arms and watched as he landed lightly on the road in front of me. Through my gasping and my watering eyes, I saw him approach and sit patiently in front of me.

He stayed in front of me with that cool patience that is signature to cats, waiting as I caught my breath.

"Thanks, pal. You saved my life back there."

Fox groomed his whiskers with a paw, casually acknowledging my debt to him.

And there's the thing.

This cat could have made an easy escape from the re-animates. He could have run to a safe place, or he could have climbed a tree with virtually no exertion. He could have taken himself out of harm's way with no effort at all.

But he hadn't. Instead, he had warned me and he had let me pick him up and run for mile after jostling mile, making no attempt to escape.

He had chosen to stay with me, and I have no idea why.

I am left to wonder at the actions of this small fellow who had chosen me as a friend. What could have possessed him to do such a thing, to make such a decision?

I reached out to Fox and rubbed a spot just behind his ear, watching his eyes close in the expression of feline luxury.

"What made you stick around, little buddy? What the hell were you thinking?"

Fox sat there and purred, and that was all the answer he gave.

The Oklahoma/Colorado Border
The Silence of the Grave

I have been thinking about my latest encounter with the re-animates, how Fox and I barely escaped with skin and fur intact, and I am reminded of something that happened shortly after the outbreak of the plague.

It's another in a long string of disturbing things about the undead, as if being dead and still walking around wasn't disturbing enough.

Shortly after I left Florida, I ran into a situation where the re-animates weren't moaning or silently moving, they were doing something that was way more unnerving.

They were standing, in a group, at a little spot by the side of the road, still as statues.

I was nearly past them when I noticed them, but they had seen me.

All heads were turned in my direction as they tracked me through sightless eyes, yet they never moved a muscle or uttered a whisper of noise.

They stood there, still and silent. Yet for all the world they looked like they were aware, watching. That occasion was the first of what have been only a few encounters. These are rare, thank you God and Mr. Poe, because they damn sure chill my blood.

When the undead are so totally motionless, yet so obviously aware of you, that's about as unsettling as it gets.

In those times, I ask myself if they are at long last running out of energy, like a toy whose batteries have finally begun to drain. Or is it something else?

Are they waiting for something?

I try not to think about it too much. A decent night's sleep is hard enough to come by as it is. There's no sense deliberately making it more difficult.

December
Year Two of the Plague
The Colorado Border
Winter Camp, and Meeting Ranger

There is the taste of winter in the air, and I find myself the heir to good fortune.

I had been searching for a camp, with the onset of winter in mind, ever since leaving Tennessee. I am farther north than I've ever been, so finding a secure place to settle has been essential. Having spent my life in Florida, and with most of my travels confined to the lower Gulf Coast, I am keenly aware of how little I know about dealing with the colder season.

I've gotten to be very good at camping, but I'm still nowhere near good enough to hold out against the cold in nothing more than a tent. So, in scouting a place to settle, I have been looking for more permanent structures. My luck was better than I could have hoped.

My winter quarters are in a small, secluded neighborhood that was part of a once well-to-do area nestled in one of those cul-de-sacs that are familiar in every part of the country. The house I chose is a solid one, still standing secure and uncorrupted. There are no signs that this home was subject to any break-ins, looting, or the depredations by the re-animates. The entire neighborhood, for that matter, appears to be in excellent condition, given all the time it has lain abandoned. As a bonus, the house I selected has a roof equipped with solar tiles. So does the house adjacent to it. The tiles still work, and the household batteries are fully charged.

There is a small strip shopping center a handful of miles from my quarters, more good fortune, and Fox and I have spent the last couple of weeks ferrying canned goods from its grocery store to our winter home. The shopping center, with the exception of its island gas station, is also virtually untouched. Fox and I will have plenty of stores to tide us over when winter lays siege to this area.

It is strange to see the strip center untouched even though the gas station was clearly ransacked and left open to the elements. It's not the first time I've seen something like this, and I'm hard-pressed to find any answer that makes sense. About the only thing that comes to mind is the fact that the locals must have thought the situation was desperate, and they were determined to leave with the clothes on their backs and the gas in their tanks. That may, or may not, have been how things were. But it's all I have to explain how the gas station could be so completely wrecked while other stores, less than a stone's throw away, could be so completely untouched.

Fox, for his part, appeared quite happy to learn that our supplies included several bags of dry cat food. I suspect that he appreciates the variety in his diet and welcomes the crunchy food as an addition to the fire-cooked game. Or he may just be tired of my cooking. Whichever it is, I'm just glad that my new traveling companion is happy with it.

That brings me to what has become a growing list of peculiarities. The cat food, though slightly musty, still seems surprisingly fresh. And it shouldn't be. That food has been on the store shelves since the outbreak of the plague, and the store has been without any power for just as long. The cat food, and everything else on the store shelves, should have been long gone by now, but it has survived remarkably well. The fresh meats, along with the fruits and vegetables, have all gone to spoilage, but it's spoilage that looks more like weathering. Time appears to have largely ignored the canned and packaged goods. I have wracked my brains for an explanation, but I haven't got a thing.

Yet, while I don't know what's keeping the food in as good condition as it is, I'm not complaining. Providence, if you're listening, I'm saying thank you.

Food for humans, cats, and dogs will be plentiful this winter.

Yeah. About the dog food. I seem to have picked up another traveling companion.

I had been setting up stores of fresh-caught game, mostly deer, to supplement the canned goods I had stockpiled, when this fellow ambled into the neighborhood. I was canning and jerking deer meat in a small clearing near my winter camp, figuring I would want plenty of stores on hand in case the winter might turn hard, when a dog strolled up and sat down. Like Fox, he moved with the casual assumption that he owned the place and was right at home here, thank you very much.

Fox glanced at the dog, hissed, and went back to looking at me.

I looked over at the dog.

"Be right with you, I'm just at a delicate place here."

It takes three hours for water at a steady boil to help ensure something is properly canned, and I was close to that point with the deer meat. I didn't want to mess anything up and ruin my stocks, so I kept my attention on my fire, the large kettle filled with boiling water, and the sealed cans that were jostling and simmering. The dog waited patiently for me to finish, blissfully unaware of the black looks he was getting from Fox.

Once I was confident everything had been boiled properly, I took the kettle off the fire and turned to the dog. He had seemed friendly enough, so that had set me a puzzle I wanted to answer right away. I had never heard of a wild dog being friendly and approaching a human; but, then again, I had never heard of that being the case with a wild cat, and I had the example of Fox to remind me I was in a world where the old rules might no longer apply at all. Still, with this new arrival, I wanted to make sure that nature hadn't thrown me any new curves.

The first order of business was to make sure this dog was healthy. Checking him as best as I knew how, I saw his eyes were bright, his ears seemed to be okay and alert to vagrant sounds, his teeth looked good. Healthy gums, wet nose, all signs of a dog who was in good physical condition.

Then I found the collar.

It was a simple, olive-colored affair, made of heavy canvas. A metal loop held a name tag in place. On the tag was stamped a series of numbers and a name: "Ranger."

I sat back on my haunches and tried to process what I had just discovered, and what the implications of that discovery could be. It was a lot to take in, more than I'd had to absorb at one time since the beginning of this plague. In a world filled with the undead, the most stunning thing was this dog tag.

And dog tag was what it was, literally. I had recognized the digits on it. They were a U.S. Army serial number. Ranger had been someone's K-9 partner, and recently. His tag wasn't some crude cobbled-together article, either. This had been machined and engraved with precision. Someone had machines, skill, electricity, and time enough to do a proper job. Nothing else could explain this engraving.

The whole thing, the manufactured collar, the tag with the name and serial number, all pointed to an organized establishment, and I was willing to bet it was military in nature. It might have been national guard or regular Army, but it was an outfit that had military discipline down to a fine art. Ranger's bearing and attitude, the way he obeyed even a casual command, all of it implied a high level of professional training. Someone had taken a great deal of time and effort here and had exercised an incredible amount of patience and care with this animal.

And, for some reason, they had let him go ... left him to fend for himself.

That was the part that didn't add up.

No professional soldier would cut his partner loose in what amounted to a wilderness, leaving him to rely on his own instincts and nothing else. For any soldier, that would be unthinkable.

Unless the alternative was worse.

There was no doubt that Ranger had been part of an organized military unit, and Ranger and his partner had been in this area recently. Something must have happened that was straight out of hell.

But what? And what about Ranger's people?

Had Ranger been part of a small unit, or a larger one? It struck me that, if Ranger had been part of a large unit, any contact with another large force would have raised the devil's own ruckus. Given the silent nature of this world, I was willing to bet that there would have been some attention-getting heavy gunfire. Yet I had heard nothing during my long approach to this area.

So, scratch that idea.

it seemed more likely that Ranger had been part of a small patrol, or Ranger and his partner may have been scouts who ran into trouble. Regardless of which it was, the thought that there might be something hostile literally in my neighborhood was plenty sobering. I was going to add to my alarms and defenses, like tonight.

But two things were clear. The first was that Ranger had been part of a well-organized and professional group, and I was willing to bet that group still existed. The name tag, the serial number, and evident training all argued in favor of a substantial level of organization and bureaucracy.

I was not alone. There were others, and Ranger's disposition told me they were friendly.

The second thing that was clear … we weren't going anywhere any time soon. Winter was coming fast, and it would be suicidal to be on the road and exposed if something like a snowstorm hit. We had to stay where we were and ride things out. The job of finding Ranger's unit was going to have to wait. There was no other choice.

I scratched Ranger behind his ear.

"Well, fellow, I don't know where you've been or what you've gone through, but you can team up with us if you like. We'll find your people as soon as the weather breaks."

I looked over to Fox.

"Looks like we have a new member of the team, little pal."

Fox glared for a moment, then seemed to resign himself to the fact that Ranger was now a member of the crew.

But I would have sworn he sighed audibly.

December
The Colorado Border
Winter, and Winter Lights

The winter cold, long expected, arrived this week. Snow came along with the cold, blanketing everything in sheer white and seeming to add an extra layer of silence to it all. The good news is that the snow sweeps easily enough from the solar tiles of the house, so I can take advantage of any stray light that penetrates the clouds. The household batteries have plenty of storage, but I still want to keep a strong margin for safety.

I'm glad I made preparations for this season, securing a house to serve as a camp and making sure supplies are adequate for what could be a months-long siege against the elements. Blankets were found in abundance in this house, along with an electric space heater that, thankfully, still works. I'm only using the downstairs, setting up a cot for myself and blankets for Fox and Ranger. The upstairs is secured and locked, windows shuttered tight, and doors safely closed.

The arrangement is sensible and cozy. The three of us only need the downstairs. By keeping things this way, we're making the most efficient use of space and resources. We have power for the little luxuries, like heat and the occasional warm meal cooked on a stove. The boys are happy enough with things, as long as they can get outdoors to do what they need to do, then get back inside and curl up on their blankets.

Fox has decided that Ranger isn't so bad a companion after all, especially since he generates dog-amounts of warmth. He has taken to sleeping alongside Ranger, who deals with this new development with the patience only a dog can muster.

I suppose it was watching the two of the boys, sound asleep and peaceful, that led me to do something I'd never have considered otherwise.

It all began with a string of lights I found in the attic.

I had been looking for any camping gear that might have been stowed in the attic when I found several strings of them stored with other holiday decorations. Acting on a wild impulse, I grabbed up all the lights I could find.

Over the next couple of days, with the boys tagging along, I strung the lights across porches and fronts of houses, hooking everything up to the battery in the house next door to ours.

Tonight, for the first time, I switched them on.

From inside the house, the boys and I watched the lights, brilliant against the snow that covered the ground.

It isn't lost on me that there is nobody nearby who can see these lights. We are alone in this neighborhood ... and we may well be the only living things for hundreds of miles.

But none of that seems to matter. I stand at the window, looking out at the lights. The boys sit beside me, regarding the lights with the same calm.

"Well, boys, what do you think?"

My voice is softer than I remember it, but I like it more this way. It seems better suited to this quieter world, and to the peaceful nature of this evening.

Winter settles around our camp, with its lights strung against the dark. I know the thaw will come, and we will break camp. Somewhere out there, hopefully along our path, we may be able to find Ranger's people. Between us and them, however, may be untold numbers of re-animates, or things even worse. We will see, in time.

For now, though, it's good to spend a peaceful night with the boys.

Christmas is coming, and for the first time since I can remember, I have friends to share it with.

Colorado Winter Camp
April and May
Year Two of the Plague
Teaching the Boys

It's April now, and based on my calculations, probably a couple of days away from May. I've been keeping track of the days through my old-fashioned way of ticking them off in my laptop's notebook. It's low-tech, but does the job well enough. My computer's date-keeping system settled down after some trouble-shooting on my end, but I still don't trust it. I suspect my glitch from last summer fouled things up for keeps, so it's a good thing I started date-keeping with the hash-marks in my notebook. I'm willing to bet I'm not off by more than a couple of weeks.

We have spent more time in this winter camp than I had planned at first, but it has been time invested wisely. I've been working with Fox and Ranger, teaching the boys something of tactics and commands for when we get back on the road and start looking for Ranger's people. We've been at work since December, and I've enjoyed the time spent in teaching my buddies and getting to know them better. Soon, however, it'll time for us to break camp and move on. Ready or not.

The teaching has gone surprisingly well, thanks to an old manual I was able to find. The handbook was neglected, back in the stacks of a bookstore at the shopping center I've been pillaging for supplies. There was a wealth of information about hand signals, which Ranger seemed to recognize immediately. His responses to them have been alarmingly good, and he has even picked up on some signals I've tried to modify to suit our circumstances. After all, there was nothing in the handbook about fighting the undead. Ranger has adapted well.

Fox is the partner who has really surprised me. I knew Ranger had substantial military training, and I'd hoped it had stuck with him. Fox, on the other hand, presented me with the altogether unexpected. He was a wild thing, feral for all his approachability, and I was unsure if he would show any interest in learning signs, commands, and basic strategies like those I had been teaching Ranger. My experience with cats had always taught me that they would do what they wanted, and only what they wanted.

It turns out Fox wanted to learn how to be a better hunter.

Fox has taken the commands I've taught him and added them to the instincts of an apex predator, finely honed over evolutionary generations. Despite his relatively small size, he has shown an almost disturbing level of ability. I believe, if it came down to it, this twenty-five pound cat could disable or critically wound a full-grown human.

Ranger has become the soldier at the full peak of his training, and Fox has become the most lethal of predators. The three of us have become a unit. For the first time since I began my travels, I believe there is a real chance of reaching our destination in Colorado.

This brings me to a line of thinking that has cost me more than one night of sleep, as I find myself confronting new ideas and getting lost in the wonder of their implications. The boys are very good with their education, so good that I can't call any of this training. I sense there is more to it than that.

The boys don't just obey simple commands. They follow complex routines that can involve multiple sets of instructions. They follow these routines, and sometimes they improvise. This means more than mere training. Memory is at work here. Comprehension is at work.

The boys know how to follow commands and apply existing knowledge to solving new problems. They know how to analyze a situation and either follow a given routine or invent a new one.

They are thinking. At least, I believe they are.

In all fairness, this is the place where I admit my own knowledge of the ways of cats and dogs is limited. For all I know, this is how these animals always have reacted to training. I may be seeing the same thing that animal trainers have seen a million times before in a million different situations. This may be something that is neither new nor unique.

Or maybe not.

Maybe there is something going on here, after all. Maybe, just maybe, a change in circumstances has nudged something dormant in these animals.

Maybe something has been sleeping in the minds of cats and dogs for uncounted evolutionary ages, and now it's waking up.

Colorado Winter Camp
Late May
Year Two of the Plague
Random Thoughts

We are preparing to break winter camp and start on the road to Cheyenne Mountain. If all goes well, the back roads will get us there before summer's end. It is strange to realize that the goal of this journey is so close as to feel tangible. This is no longer an abstraction, a name circled on a map. It's a real place, and we are getting closer to it.

I wonder what kind of a world will meet the three of us when we get to our destination and call it journey's end. Will we find Ranger's people, working to restore civilization? Will we find the rebuilding already well on the way with us being among the last to learn of it?

Or will we find nothing but emptiness and ruin, as I have found countless times before?

Will every place be overrun by the undead?

Those are the questions that can drive me to distraction if I let them. I know that one way or another, I'll have my answers soon enough.

Still, it can be hard to shake the feeling of loneliness and isolation that has been a companion for far too long. It makes me grateful for the company of Fox and Ranger. They may be a cat and a dog respectively, but they are companions and reminders that I am not the only living thing in this world.

And maybe Ranger's people are out there where we can find them. That gives me hope.

Besides, this isn't the first time the world has come to an end.

It has happened many times before.

In books, radio plays, and movies, the world has ended time and again.

Authors, singlehandedly or in collaboration with teams of actors and writers have made this happen. They have brought the world to a cataclysmic end and sometimes they have accomplished this within the span of an hour or two.

They have summoned legions of invaders from distant planets and called them to decimate the population of Earth and destroy its cities.

The military, civilian science, all the world's most powerful institutions found themselves helpless in the grip of an invading force as relentless as the tide.

All we could do is watch or listen helplessly, or read of these world-ending catastrophes voraciously.

But at the end of the day, they were all just novels or flickering images on a screen. We could put the books away or walk out of the theaters thinking about what we had just witnessed.

We could turn these ideas over and over in our minds, wondering what it might be like if the world were to end and all of humanity's works were to fail against invasion or natural calamity.

Sometimes we would watch these dramas and think of a world cut down by our own devices. Would war or ecological suicide be our undoing?

Or would the agent be a virus?

I think of this because I used to enjoy reading these books and watching these movies during that most frightening month: October. I would enjoy these stories and I would shiver at some of them, and the next day I would wake up and go to work in an ordinary world.

And our world ended in the month of October; and I'm fairly sure that there will be no waking up and going back to work this time.

No, this time the end came with no chance of business as usual the next day.

Now the horror is all too real.

And it was October ... how long ago? ... that the microorganism we came to know as the Argus/Jones virus began its plague-like spread across our world. Within the span of that month, we saw people become infected, fall ill, and die from this microscopic enemy.

Then we saw them rise and walk again.

We had never seen a disease that killed all that it infected, and then robbed them of the mercy of the grave.

We had never known an illness that could destroy a living human, then use the animated remains as a relentless vector to spread and infect others.

There had been stories, buried deep in folktales and legends. They had been the stuff of myth and tales told around late-burning fires ... perhaps from the time when humans first learned to harness that rare element and use it to hold the night at arm's length.

Perhaps we should have paid more attention to those stories. Perhaps we should have listened to these cautionary tales of our ancestors. Perhaps we should have been less ready to dismiss all this as folklore.

Or perhaps there is nothing we could have done at all.

It may be that this disease had been with us all along, dormant until some genetic switch was thrown, or some planetary balance tipped ... or until the laws of chance rolled in favor of the nearly impossible.

I honestly don't know.

But I know that this plague came upon us in the month of October, the month that brought so many stories that were once left on darkened screens or between the covers of closed books.

And I know that Octobers have come and gone since then, though I wonder how much that truly matters. The days, as we used to keep them, seem almost incidental to the task of living from one sunrise to the next. The calendar holds about it an air of unreality.

Are there any others out there, people rebuilding our civilization who might take note of the passage of time; who might organize the progression of days and months? Or does any thought of this end with me?

I wonder at times if there will be anything at all in Colorado Springs. Will I reach an enclave of civilization or another dead end? Another ghost town?

Am I only chasing phantoms?

Is mine a fool's errand?

This rumination makes my thoughts turn to scenes from the books or the movies where the lone and lonely reach out in the slim hope of contact with somebody, with anybody.

Before the Internet, there was the radio; the high magic of its day. There were the spells and summons cast over the wireless and into the invisible medium. There were call-signs and words that beckoned. One stands out from memory. It was the call to someone called "CQ."

I learned that "CQ" was an invitation for anybody on that frequency to respond, anybody at all. Sometimes the radio operator might be of a mind to chat with some friend waiting to be made.

Sometimes the person at the radio might want nothing more than to know that someone else is out there, that night and the hiss of static weren't all that remained of the world.

I wish this was all just another story and that the morning would dawn bright with all the nightmare shadows fading.

But I know that tomorrow, when it arrives, will see me waking up in a world where the dead walk and the living are all but gone.

And I wonder if Fox, Ranger, and I may be among the last of the living. I wonder if this has now become a world where nothing is left but the dead untethered to the grave.

Hello, it's me, Jake. I'm here. I'm alive. ... Calling CQ ...

Do you read me, CQ? Do you read me?

... Anybody?

Colorado
June
Year Two of the Plague
Bird-Watching

We saw carrion birds today.

The boys and I were on the road, steadily making our way toward that spot on the map that said, "Cheyenne Mountain." We'd been dutifully keeping to the back roads that have been a staple of my travels when we noticed the birds. They were circling an area probably only a few miles ahead of us. It looked like they'd found an enclave of the re-animates.

I've seen this before.

Vultures will circle over individuals or a crowd of re-animates, sometimes circling for hours, then they will fly away. The carrion birds don't try to dip low and investigate, and I've never seen them settle and peck at the undead. They leave those corpses alone, whether they are shambling or whether they have collapsed and stopped moving altogether.

It's as if these birds know the difference between the undead and the truly dead. They've adapted and will feed on the dead despite the obvious lack of decay in corpses these days. But the undead, the re-animates? They won't go near them.

That tracks with something I have noticed about the way animals react to the undead. They have a deep, gut-level hatred of the things and they don't mind expressing it.

In Florida, during the outbreak of the plague, I saw police dogs barely held in check as they snarled and snapped at the undead. Their jaws were slathered with saliva and their eyes hyper-focused on the re-animates that were just out of reach.

Neighborhood cats would hiss and spit at the undead, growling and sometimes menacing them in packs. Driving them off. That's been the only time I've ever seen anything like self-preservation in the re-animates, when the cats go after them.

In the Florida panhandle, I saw a black bear repeatedly bellow and cuff one of the re-animates. The animal literally slapped at the creature till it disintegrated. The bear didn't stop until there was nothing left of the re-animate except for scattered pieces. Then, apparently finished, the bear ambled away.

It's as though the animals, wild and domesticated alike, sense that the undead are a violation of the natural order, and it drives them to an insane fury. Or as is the case with the carrion birds, it makes them treat the undead with a contemptuous disregard.

In either event, the animals show no fear. For them, it's either attack or ignore, with no other options.

Only humans fear the undead.

Colorado
July
Year Two of the Plague
The Last Man on Earth?

I need to put some disturbing thoughts into this journal here, because if I don't they'll eat me alive. If, by some miracle, you are alive and reading what I'm writing here, I just want you to know that I hate to dump everything on you like this.

But I need to put these words out where I can see them because if they stay inside my head they will destroy me. And a part of me really wants to live and learn if my journey has been worthwhile.

It's time for a true confession from me. I've been taking a long time to get from Florida to Colorado because I've been moving with an excess of caution. I've seen too many re-animates to want to end up like them. Slow and steady can save your life. It has saved mine more than once.

But I'm also moving slowly because some days it has been hard to move at all. Some days I haven't seen the sense of it.

And some days I move slowly because I no longer recognize this world. Some days I'm afraid of it, so afraid that I don't want to move. I only want to hide from this place and hope that it goes away.

I am moving through a world that is alien to the one where I grew up. This literally could not be more foreign if it were another planet. I walk through ruins that might as well be all that remains of an elder civilization, where wreckage speaks with a mute language of wonders and achievements now overgrown with weeds and the rust of decay. There are none left to tell the deeds of this civilization or those who peopled it.

Sometimes I imagine myself to be an astronaut who explores the corpse of a fallen world, pondering what might have brought it down. Only there is no ship waiting for me and there will be no stories for me to tell, because the empty world is my own.

And I know what brought it down.

And I know that there may be none left alive, but there are still those who walk this Earth.

How would an alien visitor feel upon finding this world in this condition? What would that visitor feel as the slow realization dawned that this is a planet where death is not the final word? Would they study this place and ask the questions that science works to answer? Or would they get back in their ship and escape from this world with terror nipping at their heels? Would they run and leave this planet to the undead?

And to the last living man?

And, lord, what if that's what I am? What if the ranks of the living have thinned to the point that I'm all that's left? What if the people I've had to kill on my journey were my only hope for human companionship? What if the only people who could have been company are now in graves because I put them there?

What if I'm alone and have only myself to blame for it? Those are the questions that have nagged at me and nibbled at my sense of being helpless in the face of, well, everything.

In the early days of my journey I was too busy trying to stay alive to spend any time on thoughts like this, and that may be a saving grace. Before I met Fox and Ranger, I barely had time to think about the weight of loneliness, let alone to dwell on it.

If I'd had the kind of time to let the loneliness eat at me then the way it tries to now, I would have used one of my last bullets on myself. That would have been that. Despair and emptiness would have carried the day and I would have been finished with my struggle; finished with everything.

Even now, the temptation exists. The voice is there that whispers how easy it would be to let go of it all. Just one brief blinding flash, and nothing but peace to follow after it.

Only now I know the voice belongs to a damned liar. Thanks to Fox, Ranger, and whatever put them in my path.

The boys may have saved my life, and not for the first time.

Ranger's people may still be out there, and they may be an outpost of civilization. They may be a sign that I am not alone, that there is somebody either trying to rebuild this world or at least hold it together.

That's a hope that I keep a grip on. Some days that grip is strong and secure. Some days it feels like I'm grasping at straws. But I'll still hold onto that hope and not let go.

The boys give me hope and that gives me strength, and I could sure use it.

I'm going to need it.

Something tells me the worst of this world is not yet behind me.

If you are out there to read these words and you've been feeling that sense of hopelessness or despair which has dogged me from time to time, now you know you're not alone. In more ways than one, you are *not* alone. Hang in there.

We'll get through this.

Colorado
August/September
Year two of the Plague
The Slavers and the Slaves

We smelled the slavers long before we saw them.

The boys and I were taking a detour from our path through southeastern Colorado when we literally smelled something that wasn't right. The scent made us stop where we were and stay perfectly still while we thought things through. There was more in the smell than unwashed bodies. There was the scent of neglect and things left in their own filth. And I could swear I smelled fear.

The wind had carried the stench from a position I reckoned to be about a half mile away, corresponding to the location of a major road. At least, that's what my maps told me, and they hadn't lied to me yet. I felt a touch of vindication here, an affirmation of my old decision to keep to the back roads, keep out of sight, and keep safe.

This wasn't the first time that my decision had spared me from trouble, and I was thankful for the habit. Ironically, I'd chosen my "back roads only" strategy as a way to avoid cluttered and backed-up highways early in the plague. The decision seemed to be the best way to make progress. In time, it became second nature.

Something about this just felt off. I sensed a need to take a closer look into things, though for the life of me I could not say why. I hunkered down beside Fox and Ranger.

"Well, boys, do you think maybe we should see what's going on behind that stench over there?"

Fox and Ranger didn't move, but they glanced toward the smell, then turned and looked steadily at me.

"Yeah, that's what I thought, too. Let's stay quiet and stay out of sight, but let's go take a look."

We began moving toward the stench, and soon, the sound of voices.

The whole thing had my nerves keyed tight, and I could see that the boys had their hackles up, so we worked to close our distance slowly. We were going to take our time studying this group before we made our presence known, if we chose to do so at all. I wanted to have the option to scout the group then fade back into the shadows if that looked like the best course of action.

These people might be friends, or they might be people I'd never want to meet in a dark alley. Until I knew which they were, I was not going to take chances with any premature introductions. Long experience had reinforced an old truism, so I was choosing "safe" over "sorry."

We came to a stop a fair distance from the group, on a wooded rise above them, properly concealed from sight. I'd chosen this route in hopes of getting to a place where we'd be able to observe the group as it passed. I'd be able to watch from the shadows through my binoculars and take the measure of these people, and nobody would be any the wiser. I unshipped my binoculars and waited for the group to come into view.

What I saw both sickened me and brought my blood to a boil. Three men were leading the group. At least, they might have been men once, though I had a feeling those days were long gone. They looked more like brutes a half step above the ladder from apes. They were filthy, with scraggly hair and long, ragged beards. Their clothing was even dirtier than they were and all three of them were carrying slung rifles; civilian models of military weapons, from the look of them. All told, it added up to an ugly bunch of people.

Behind them, shambling in a ragged bunching, was a group of maybe twenty men and women, all of them linked together in a chain of coarse-woven rope, and all of them completely nude. They were cleaner than their captors, but they had the look of the tired and the beaten about them. They were plodding one foot in front of the other, not daring to look up or look around.

I had never seen slaves before, but I had no doubt I was looking at them now.

Two men, both armed, brought up the rear of the caravan, with a third man trailing a substantial distance behind them. I figured the guy at the tail end of the group was there to pick up on anything the others might miss, whatever it might be. I could hear the laughter and the jokes the slavers were throwing back and forth about who they were going to pick to "keep warm tonight," and I could see the shudders and frightened glances from the slaves. Listening to this, I worked to keep calm through clenched teeth.

I kept silent, just one shadow out of many, as the group passed by and moved out of sight. I wasn't worried about finding them again. I could always follow the stench and the noise. If I needed to track them down, that would take me right to them.

And that brought me to my next question. What the hell was I going to do about this?

I figured I had two choices. I could either fade back and resume my trip toward Cheyenne Mountain, or I could try to take these bastards down.

On the one hand, I could be on my merry way and spend the rest of my life with a conscience that would dog me while I learned to sleep with one eye open. On the other hand, I could make a plan to kill these thugs and run the risk of getting cut down in the process. There were only six of the slavers, but they were six men armed with high-powered rifles. I had only my bow and arrows and the sweet light of Jesus in my eyes.

Oh sure, I totally had this covered.

While I was confident that I could strike from the shadows and kill six men before they knew what was happening, I knew it would be a completely different case with six men who'd be armed and shooting at me. That would be a good way to get killed fast. The smarter course, the one that would give me a better chance of living longer, would be to leave and do my best to forget everything I saw.

As my ex-wife would have said, I was never known for being smart.

I sat back on my haunches and looked at Fox and Ranger.

"Gentlemen, we need a plan."

Colorado

Reconnaissance

There are some things that a person can't allow to stand, as long as they have a breath in them. The risks don't matter, the odds against you don't matter, even the question of survival itself doesn't matter. Some things just can't be permitted to continue. I had found one of those things the moment that Fox, Ranger, and I had come in contact with the slaver convoy.

We had approached the convoy in absolute silence and secrecy, and none of the slavers knew we were aware of them. They had about twenty slaves, give or take a couple, and we could have let the whole crew pass along to their eventual destination. They would never have known that we had been there, watching. We could have slipped away without them being any the wiser.

Only we couldn't.

Like I said, there are some things a person can't allow to stand.

We spent the next two days observing the slavers and looking for any weak points that we could exploit and turn into a plan of attack. Through it all, though, there was something that continued to bother me, something that nagged at my thoughts. The slavers were making enough racket to wake the dead, and that wasn't just a figure of speech. The noise should have drawn every re-animate within a mile, only nothing had shambled its way to the camp. That was a loose end, and I don't like loose ends. I wanted an answer and I intended to get one before I made a move.

The next morning I got my wish. I woke up from my hiding place early and saw two unkempt creatures heading down the road toward the main camp. They must have come from a position that was miles, maybe days, farther up the road than the main group of slavers. That could explain how I missed them when I first sighted the group. I'd based my approach to the slavers on sound, so I would have focused on where the noise was coming from. An advance team could have gotten past my notice easily. I'd never gotten close enough to make out facial features and never seen what looked like a changing of the guard. These guys could have changed places once a day and I'd never have known. None of this made me feel better about my powers of observation.

I stayed still and listened to the new arrivals as they spoke with the leader of the convoy. The conversation was distant and low, but I was able to hear it well enough. I learned plenty, too. The newcomers spoke about "dealing with the dead dummies" and how the roads had stayed mostly clear since they had last come this way. They said they hadn't run into "much trouble to speak of" and were willing to bet there was only a handful of the undead wandering around between here and their destination. They figured the next advance team would be able to handle things the rest of the way back to the compound.

The leader listened, nodded, and motioned two slavers over to the smaller group. The slavers and the new arrivals spoke with the leader for a few minutes, then everybody seemed to come to some kind of agreement. It sounded like the plan was for the new team of scouts to take up position two days ahead of the convoy and keep the road clear. That would let the main group focus on keeping the slaves in line without having to worry about "the dead dummies," as they called them.

The leader shouted instructions back to the convoy and a couple of slavers ran up carrying full packs. They handed these off to the slavers who were already with the leader and the returning scouts.

The slavers shouldered their packs and handed their rifles over to the scouts. In exchange, they got what the scouts had been carrying: a couple of axes. Then, places swapped, the slavers began heading up the road, assuming their position as the new advance scouting team.

I thought about what I had just witnessed. It was interesting and damned puzzling at the same time. Why were the slavers sending their scouts out with items that were better suited to dealing with lumber than dealing with re-animates? Sure, the main camp was likely to make more noise, but those guys had looked plenty well-armed. They could have spared the extra firepower for the scouts. It didn't make sense to send them ahead with no more gear than a pair of woodcutters.

The only way this made sense was if the slavers were true believers, convinced that they had no more than a few re-animates to deal with. If they were sure that they only had to worry about a handful of the undead, then two men with axes would be up to the job. The scouts would be safe enough.

But accidents happen. Especially if someone can arrange them.

I motioned to Fox and Ranger. The three of us started to quietly maneuver ahead of the scouts. In the back of my mind, an idea was taking shape and turning into a plan.

Colorado, Oklahoma, and Back Again
Elimination of the Slaver Scouts

The boys and I spent the next few days getting ahead of the slavers' advance scouts and making sure that they would have more trouble than they could handle. If we could take these bastards at their word, then there might be six or seven re-animates between the convoy and the main camp. The two advance scouts would be able to handle them one or two at a time but not all at once.

We got to work ruining the odds for the slavers.

We had reached the border of Oklahoma and Texas when we got lucky, which meant that life was about to suck for the slaver advance team. I'd sent Ranger ahead with silent instructions to play sheepdog and round up as many re-animates as he could find, and he carried out his instructions brilliantly. I was impressed. He'd overcome his instinctive drive to attack the re-animates and had driven them to our position just ahead of the slaver scouts.

Ranger had found the first handful of the undead and had gotten their attention with a bit of barking. He was good. I could barely hear him from my position a handful of hours down the road, but I could hear the low whistling moan of the re-animates clearly.

And I heard the moaning growing louder as more dry lungs joined in.

By the time Ranger had trotted back to where Fox and I were waiting, a baker's dozen of re-animates were coming up the road, shuffling toward the last place they heard any sound. The boys and I faded away from the road and out of sight. We hunkered down and waited.

Sure enough, we soon heard the slaver scouts strolling up the road, chatting away like they were expecting only one or two re-animates at a time. They had no idea that every one of the undead between them and their destination had gathered on the road ahead of them and were shambling their way.

We kept silent and observant as reality caught up with the scouts.

By the time the slaver scouts realized there was something wrong, there wasn't a damn thing they could do about it. They were face to face with the re-animates. All that was left was the choice of close-quarters combat or cut and run. A person with a gun or other ranged weapon could have run and then turned to pick off the re-animates at their leisure. A person armed with an ax didn't have that option. That person only had the options of "stand and fight" or "turn and run like hell." In the time it took the slavers to figure that out, option two had expired.

I watched as the slavers swung their axes, desperately trying to thin the ranks of the undead. I could tell they were fighting a losing battle from the outset. It wasn't because of the numbers of re-animates. It was because of panic. The slavers had reacted out of raw instinct, and that instinct was going to kill them.

They flailed without pattern or plan, hacking at trunks, limbs, anything. Not once did the slavers aim for the head. Sometimes in their frenzy they came frighteningly close to injuring each other. I watched, darkly amused by the fact that it seemed the re-animates were fighting a more coordinated attack than the slavers.

Eventually the slavers realized that, even maimed and mutilated, the re-animates were going to keep coming, so they turned to attempt an escape. By then, it was way too late. The undead had them surrounded. I heard swearing and screaming as the slavers tried to fight their way through. They were failing, and failing in the most bloody and miserable way possible.

I might have felt sorry for their situation if I hadn't worked so hard to create it.

In the end, the slavers actually managed to finish off the re-animates, but I wouldn't call it a victory. Both men had been bitten horribly. One of them was lying in the road, chewed so badly that he looked like a pile of bloody meat. The other slaver was binding his injuries as best as he could. He was swearing and sobbing as he worked to stop from bleeding through his bandages. He was a goner and he knew it.

I stood up from my hiding place and put myself in plain sight of the man. I smiled and nodded at him. He looked up at me and his jaw dropped.

He was still staring, open-mouthed, when my arrow went through his skull.

Colorado
Attack on the Slaver Convoy

We double-timed it back to the main body of the slaver convoy. We'd been a couple of days ahead of the pack and I wanted us to get back there before the lead savers had a chance to stumble across their late companions. I wanted the slavers to be convinced that their scouts were still far ahead of them and hot on the job. The more confident they felt, the less cautious they would be.

The boys and I were able to make up a day's worth of travel in a little over eight hours, which was better timing than I had expected. Along the way, I had put together a plan that would make the best use of our talents and resources against a superior force. If those jackals were half as lax as I expected them to be, we had a really good chance against them.

We were going to use a pattern as old as the wilderness and pack-hunting. We were going to start at the back and take out the last slaver in line. It would require a precision shot from my bow, but I'd be able to make it. The slaver was far enough back from the others in the rear that it would be some time before his absence was noticed. By that time, I'd have his gun and it wouldn't matter if his buddies saw me.

We moved through the underbrush above the place where I estimated the convoy would be moving the next day, then I chose a position where I could see and not be seen, checked for a clear line of sight with my bow, and settled low in the foliage and waited. Sure enough, the convoy made camp for the night within our line of sight. The slavers were close enough for us to overhear them and track their movements, and far enough away for us to be securely outside any accidental notice.

I had toyed with the idea of sneaking up on the camp during the night and picking everybody off, but I dropped that idea after a few seconds of serious thought. The slavers were alert and taking turns on watch. They had a campfire going but the sentries were facing out toward the night and the darkness. I, on the other hand, would be looking into the light of their fire. I could say good-bye to my night vision and any chance of getting off a decent shot. Even if I could make my first arrow count, they'd be all over us before I could fire again. The opportunity wasn't worth the risk.

The noise of the slavers breaking camp woke me the next morning, though sleep had been hard enough to get, anyway. The sounds from the camp, the crude laughter of men and the cries of women, had kept me awake and angry through most of the night. I consoled myself with the thought that, if everything went according to plan, it was going to be the last night these creeps would hurt anybody.

The caravan drew near me, then past me, the slavers moving with the easy confidence of people who believe they are untouchable. The slaves shuffled along with the air of the completely defeated. As grim as that was, I knew it counted in my favor. The slaves were in no position to do anything to their captors, and the slavers knew it. Where the captives moved slowly and meekly, the slavers walked with a stride that was close to a strut. That made me feel better about my chances.

There is no one more vulnerable than the person who believes they are invincible.

The caravan passed and the last man in line finally came into view, strolling along like he had all the time in the world.

He didn't, but why spoil his last minutes on Earth by telling him?

I drew my bow, took careful aim, and waited for him to come closer. He drew near, to the point where he was barely a couple of feet away from my hiding place. He could have seen me if he had bothered to look or if he had paid any attention to his surroundings at all.

I cleared my throat. His head snapped in my direction, and I loosed my arrow. It flew straight into his eye socket.

The slaver never uttered a sound. He stumbled, with a puzzled look on his face, and staggered to some tall grass by the roadside where he fell silently. I ran up to his body, retrieved my arrow from his corpse, and took his rifle.

The magazine was empty.

It had all been a bluff. The overt parade of weapons, the bullying attitude of the slavers, the casual brutality ... it had all been camouflage. This slaver didn't have any ammunition and I was willing to bet that his buddies didn't, either. It was a ruse, designed to cow the slaves, to rob them of any hope of resistance. That explained the exchange of weapons with the scouts. In this context, it all made perfect sense. Empty guns can intimidate the living, but they're worthless against the undead. The scouts had been given axes because there was nothing else to use.

That would also explain why the slaves had been stripped of all clothing. It would keep them subservient and would also eliminate the prospect of someone hiding something like a knife. That would track with a group that wanted to give the impression of being all-powerful. The slaves might suspect that their captors had no bullets, but they couldn't be sure. The slavers, however, would know without a doubt that their captives were unarmed and in no position to resist.

I hefted the empty weapon and studied the terrain. There was a gulley on the far side of the road, so I rolled the slaver's body into it, listening as the corpse tumbled through the brush, smacking against trees on the way down. I threw the gun down after him and scuffed the earth at edge of the road, making it look like someone had lost their footing. Anyone who came looking for the slaver would find the scuffed area, see the body in the gulley, and conclude that the man had lost his balance and fallen to his death.

Plan A had been to take the slaver's weapon and use it to pick off his remaining partners, either one at a time or all at once with guns blazing. Since that plan was now trash, it was time for Plan B, which was to lurk in the shadows and team up with the boys to take out the slavers. Hopefully we would be able to do it one at a time, but we'd be ready for a knock-down drag-out fight if it came to that. I was really hoping it wouldn't come to that.

I looked at Fox and Ranger and held up two fingers. Plan B it is, boys.

I moved back into the brush with the boys. Together, we waited for one of the slaver's buddies to figure out he was missing, and to come looking for him. The slavers did not disappoint.

It took about an hour for one of the slavers to come back, looking for the missing man. He was calling out the man's name and swearing that the rest of the group was going to leave him behind if he didn't hurry up and "shake a leg." The yelling stopped when the slaver found the scuffed dirt and saw the body at the bottom of the gulley.

If the man had any feelings for the loss of his fallen comrade, he didn't show them. All I noticed was a nonchalant shrug. Then the slaver leaned over to spit absently into the gulley. It didn't look like the action was connected to the dead man. I doubt the slaver gave his late buddy any thought at all.

I tapped Ranger on his back, just between his shoulders. I motioned toward the slaver and gave Ranger the silent command to attack. In an instant, the dog bounded quietly across the road. There was no sound, not even the click of claws on pavement. In the next instant Ranger launched himself into the air, forepaws outstretched and aimed squarely at the center of the slaver's back. He landed on target, hitting hard and jumping back in a heartbeat.

The slaver, still preoccupied with whatever he was thinking, never heard Ranger run and leap. When Ranger struck, the man staggered and spun on his heels, arms windmilling in the air. As he turned around, desperately trying to recover his balance, he caught sight of Ranger. Then he saw me, and he saw my bowstring drawn tight.

I'm pretty sure he saw the arrow that caught him in the chest, too. Not that there was anything he could do about it. The man uttered a short scream, then fell backward into the gulley, taking his weapon, and my arrow, with him.

Fox, Ranger, and I faded back into the trees and the low brush that had kept us hidden, and waited to see what would happen next. At this point, I wasn't sure how things would break. I didn't know if we could continue to take out the slavers one by one.

I thought about what I would do in the face of a similar situation. Two men had disappeared from the tail end of the convoy, leaving only one person to cover the rear. One disappearance could be easily interpreted as an accident, but two? If I'd been the last man in line, I would have gotten a little suspicious at that point. I would have called a halt and called up reinforcements from among the three men at the front of the convoy.

Bless the winds of fortune and the conviction of invulnerability. The idea that something fishy was happening was an idea that never crossed the third man's mind. He came trotting back, alone, to the place where his partners had vanished, as clueless and predictable as a teenager in a slasher movie.

I was able to recover my arrow this time and add his body to the growing pile of corpses at the bottom of the gulley.

Had I been in charge of the slaver convoy, my every alarm and sense of danger would be going off by now. Three of my men had gone missing in maybe a handful of hours, under circumstances that were asking too much of accident and coincidence. I would be on full alert, and I would want to make absolutely sure that it was some freak accident which had cost me those three men and nothing else. I would not want to rest until I had my answer.

Had I been in charge, I might also be realizing right about now that, no matter what I did, I was screwed.

The lead slaver could send one man back to the rear to investigate and probably join his buddies at the bottom of the gully, or he could send two men to investigate, leaving one man alone to guard the slaves. Either way, he would be exactly one man short of any plan that could offer some level of safety.

He chose to send two men back, and then he chose to do something unexpected.

The boys and I were moving silently toward the front of the convoy, keeping to our shadows, when we saw two of the slavers pass by us on the opposite side of the road. I could tell they were keyed up, because they were casting anxious looks from side to side. They couldn't see us, and they moved along without ever knowing we were there. We let them go. We were aiming for the head of the snake.

As we reached the front of the caravan, we saw the man who had to be the leader of this little group. He was holding a woman in front of him, with a gun pressed to her temple, and he was shouting for me.

"I don't know who you are, but I know you're out there! And you goddam well better make yourself seen or I'm gonna start shooting these people. I swear to God I'll do it, so you better show yourself!"

I stepped out of the shadows, my arms raised above my head. The slaver snarled a grin and turned his pistol toward me, leveling the weapon and drawing back the hammer. My right hand twitched slightly.

Ranger bolted from the brush inches from the man and struck him hard. I could hear the slaver's ribs crack from where I was standing. The man staggered back and fired, but the shot went wild.

I nearly had a heart attack when I heard the report. I had made a serious miscalculation about the state of ammunition among the slavers. At least one of them still had a loaded weapon and would have killed me if I'd been a second too late with my signal to Ranger.

All this flashed through my brain as I ran toward the man and tackled him the rest of the way to the ground. I could see pinkish foam on the slaver's lips, a sign of a punctured lung. Ranger must have hit him really hard. I noted this in the instant it took me to pull my knife and drive it into the slaver's heart. He shuddered and went still, his eyes wide. I hoped he was looking straight into hell.

I heard the pounding of boots on gravel and turned to confront the last two slavers. Clever bastards. They had feinted their trip to check on their dead partners. Instead of going all the way back to where they lost their comrades, they had circled around and come back in this direction. They were coming, one of them at a dead run, while I scrabbled at my knife, trying to pull it from the chest of the leader.

The nearer slaver was closing in on me. He was still a respectable distance away, and it wouldn't take him long to reach me, but he wasn't my problem, The man behind him was. The more distant slaver was calmly lifting his rifle and aiming along the barrel, keeping me clearly in his sights. I could see his finger on the trigger of the weapon, my eyes focused on it with an almost supernatural clarity as he began to squeeze. From the looks of things, I was going to be dead long before the first guy got to me.

Then the slaver screamed, jerking my attention away from the rifle and that finger on the trigger. The man flung the weapon away and flailed his hands toward his face, scrabbling at the bloody sockets which, a moment ago, had been his eyes. I watched, open-mouthed, as a cat that weighed maybe twenty-five pounds revealed himself as a lightning-fast predator, a flurry of fangs and razor-sharp claws, the descendant of a lineage that reached back to pre-history and the time of the saber-cats. The heir to a kingdom whose throne was the chewed bones of the defeated.

Fox was a blur around the slaver, inflicting an unholy degree of damage while never staying still for more than a second. He snapped upward, biting and raking thigh muscles with fangs and claws, then dancing back as the blinded slaver staggered around searching for a target, any target.

Fox darted in and slashed at a bloody gap in the slaver's pants leg. I heard the pop of a tendon and saw the man collapse to one knee, sobbing. Then the slaver's sobs turned to a wet gurgling, and Fox was dancing back from the ruins of the man's throat. All the slaver could do was clutch at a mass of severed veins and slashed arteries as the last moments of his life bled through his hands.

Fox settled back and observed his work cooly, licking the blood from his claws with a nearly contemptuous lack of interest in the man who was dying less than two feet away from him.

The last of the slavers had by now closed the distance to me. Bellowing, he raised his rifle butt with the clear intention of crushing my skull. He never got the chance.

None of us, not Ranger or Fox or me, could have moved fast enough to stop the slaver from bringing his rifle down on my head. The slaves, on the other hand, were a different story. They tripped him, causing him to crash headlong to the road.

One of the slaves, a woman, had a small rock gripped in each hand and I saw her pounce on the man, straddling him as much as her bonds would permit. She began a furious hammering, bringing the rocks down against the slaver's head again and again. She was chained fury, her blows landing with a rhythmic, fleshy thumping. She kept striking at the slaver long after he had stopped trying to defend himself, and long after he had stopped moving.

I stood aside and let the woman go to work on her former tormentor. Truthfully, I would have been afraid to try and stop her.

I had seen the look of murderous anger on her face; a mask of rage against tear-stained cheeks.

She didn't ease up with her blows until there was nothing but red pulp where the man once had a face. Then she rocked back, sobbing. The slaver didn't move at all, and there was no rising and falling of his chest.

I began moving from one person to the next, using my knife to cut through their bonds. They were free. It was done.

I let the huddled people stand up and rub at their wrists and ankles, restoring some circulation and easing the pain from the ropes I had recently cut. Fox and Ranger sidled up to me and sat down. The three of us waited for everyone to collect themselves and enjoy breathing free air again. After a few minutes, I cleared my throat.

"Is there someone in charge here? Someone I can speak to?"

The woman with the rocks and the bloody fists stood up and wiped at her eyes.

"That would be me."

Colorado

The Slave's Story

"How did this happen?"

The woman looked at me, not quite trusting.

"That's an interesting question. Why are you asking?"

I replied, "It would help to hear your story. I might learn what to do in case I run across something like this later."

She shrugged, "Fair enough. But can we get back to where they left our clothes? It's a few days walk, and I'd like to put something on again. Besides, the nights still get pretty damned cold around here."

I nodded," Sorry. I should have thought of that. The boys and I will go with you to make sure you get there safely."

She looked at me quizzically. "The boys?"

I tipped my head toward Fox and Ranger.

"My buddies here. The cat is Fox and the dog is Ranger."

"Are they the only ones who have names or do you have one, too?"

"My name is Jacob, but I go by Jake. How about you?"

"I'm Della, but around here they call me Dee. So your 'boys' are Fox and Ranger. They sound like interesting companions. I'd like to hear how you three got together, but we should get moving now. It's going to get dark soon, and I don't want to stay here."

We began our hike back to where the slaves had been forced to leave their clothing. Looking back the way we had come, I saw the carrion birds beginning to circle and land where the six corpses lay. I heard the distant calls of the birds settling down to feast.

Bon Appetit', fellows.

The trip back to where the slaves had been forced into bondage took eleven days and change. Over the course of those days, Dee told me about how they had met the slavers and how things had turned so terribly against their group.

The group, a collection of refugees from the early days of the outbreak, had been traveling from the midwest. According to Dee, they had planned to get far enough south for the winters to be tolerable and for them to find a place with a longer growing season. Most of the people in the group had made plans for an extended time on the road. There were only a couple of hunting rifles among them, but plenty of non-perishable supplies.

Like me, these people had started in cars, though they had traveled mostly along the main roads. The initial group, from the greater Chicago area, had met others along the way and had eventually linked up into a five-car convoy.

Also, like me, they had eventually run out of uncontaminated gas and been forced to continue on foot. Nobody had thought to pack bicycles, but I suspected that bikes wouldn't have been practical in a group that size. Maintenance had been a chore for me, traveling mostly alone. It might have been more than a larger group could realistically handle.

Dee said they had counted on the sheer size of the group to ensure their safety, and I could see her point. Bandits, if there were any lurking around, would be more inclined to attack a solitary traveler than a group that had them outnumbered. It made sense. In most situations, including encounters with re-animates, the idea of safety in numbers was solid.

This crew just hadn't counted on meeting people like the slavers.

Dee told me the slavers were genial enough when they first met them on the road. Despite their rough appearance, they were friendly, and sometimes charming, the first few days they traveled with the group. She said she figured they might be good company once they got cleaned and washed. They even apologized for being ragged and unwashed.

The slavers said they had been on a scouting job away from their community and would be glad to get back to some soap and water. They described the place as a small town that was growing, "Thanks to finding people like you." The slaver leader asked if the group was interested in traveling with them to their community and making a new home there. Naturally, everyone in the group jumped on the invitation and agreed to go along. They were thrilled by the idea as they would be finding a place where they could settle down. Compared to life on the road, it sounded like absolute paradise.

The first sign that something was wrong came two days later. A member of the group was missing, and so was all the ammunition for the hunting rifles. One of the slavers had said that he had talked with the man the night before, and that the man had mentioned a desire to "go it alone and see where the road leads." The slaver said he hadn't paid much attention to the man at the time and had shrugged it off as wistful rambling.

The explanation didn't feel right to Dee, since the man in question had been one of the group's best shots and one of the least trusting of outsiders.

Other things weren't adding up, either. The slavers kept changing their stories about the community. They weren't big changes, but they were the kind that didn't align with a place that is supposed to be well-known to its residents. The stories also changed slightly from one slaver to another. Before long, Dee was beginning to believe that the community the slavers had described was a complete work of fiction.

She spoke of her misgivings to other people in her group, quietly and in small numbers. She learned that she wasn't the only person who felt uneasy about their new associates. Over the course of the next few days, the group came to a silent decision. They would leave these new people and stay with their original plan to head south.

They still had one hunting rifle. They believed they could find ammunition before their supplies ran too low.

The morning of the group's planned departure the slavers woke them up. Their leader had a man on his knees in front of him and was holding a pistol to the man's head. The other slavers had surrounded the group, with their rifles unslung and aimed. Dee recognized the kneeling man. He had been a part of their group since the beginning, and she had spoken to him only the night before.

The slaver leader spoke to the group.

"Well, it looks like some of you aren't so happy with our friendship. And others," he cuffed the man's head, "couldn't wait to tell us all about it."

He looked over the group.

"So here's the score: you are going to do exactly what we tell you to do, when we tell you to do it, and how we tell you to do it. Or we are going to start shooting. And we're going to keep shooting till all of you fall in line."

The slaver pressed his gun against the kneeling man's head. "And, since nobody likes a snitch, we're going to start here."

Dee said with that, the slaver leader calmly squeezed the trigger and blew the man's brains out.

"They killed ten of us before we surrendered to them," she said. "Then they killed all three of our children."

If I had harbored any misgivings about what I had done to the slavers, they evaporated in that moment.

Two days after Dee had told me her story, we arrived at the place where the group had been forced to remove their clothes and assume their new lives as slaves. Dee had already confirmed my suspicions about the reason for this. The slavers straight-up told them it would make them more manageable. She said the leering gazes from the slavers had also made them stay quiet and pray they would be ignored.

I did a little math, based on what she had told me about everything, and I realized I'd launched my attack on the slavers a little less than two weeks after they had turned these people into their captives. That still meant about 12 days and nights of pure torture for these people, but there wasn't a damn thing I could do to change any of it.

No sense dwelling on those "if only" moments when you don't have a time machine to fix them.

After everyone had dressed and recovered their abandoned belongings, I helped the group make camp for the evening. When everyone had gotten settled, Dee pulled me aside to speak with me. I was not surprised by this, since we had talked quite a bit during the past few days. I'd told her all about my travels, including how I'd met up with Fox and Ranger. We had come to know each other as well as two people can in such a short time, and we felt relaxed in each other's company.

She looked at me, her head tilted critically, and ran her fingers through my hair.

"Lord, what a mess. Who does your hair, the Three Stooges?"

I deadpanned, "Nyuk nyuk nyuk."

That earned me a hearty glare and a swift command. "Sit."

"Yes, ma'am," I did exactly what she told me to.

She reached into her rucksack and pulled out a pair of scissors. Sure hands went to work on my hair, trimming things up.

"You know, it really doesn't look that bad," I said more in defense of my own work than in a legitimate attempt to change her mind.

She didn't say a word, but her trimming got more ... determined.

When she had finished, she stepped back and checked her work.

"I suppose that will have to do, though it isn't my best. Still, you look almost civilized. And you know how to trim your beard."

She rubbed at my whiskers, "Yeah, you should keep that. It works for you."

"Thanks, Dee," I grinned and may have blushed.

She looked at me thoughtfully, as if reaching a decision, "What the hell. You can call me Della."

"Della," I rolled the name on my tongue. "I like it. I like how it fits you. It's ... well ... it's pretty."

She lowered her eyes and smiled. I had never seen her smile before. I thought she looked radiant.

We went back to the rest of the group and had dinner. I made sure that watches were posted before everyone turned in for the night. Once that was done, I made my plans to leave on the next day.

That morning, I took out my maps. I gave the group directions to my winter sanctuary and described the area to them. I let them know that the place had access to the local strip mall, and that it could be fortified. I told everyone what I knew about the local edible plants, and what I knew of the growing season. All in all, I noted, this could be a secure place to regroup and perhaps a good place to settle down. I ended my presentation by handing over my earlier maps, keeping only those I would need to reach my destination.

Della checked the maps I was still holding. She saw Cheyenne Mountain circled in red.

"So you still intend to go there. You think there's hope." It was not a question.

"Yeah, but first I need to make a detour." I tapped an area on the map near the Oklahoma and Texas border. It was where the slavers had been going, according to what I had overheard from them and what Della had confirmed.

"You think you can do anything against those people?" That was definitely a question.

I shrugged. "I'll know when the boys and I see the place. Maybe there's nothing we can do. Maybe there's business we can finish. We'll just have to see."

"You rely a lot on each other."

"We're a team. Right, boys?"

Ranger wagged his tail and Fox made a big display of being disinterested.

"Wait. Stay here just a minute." She ran into the underbrush and came back a moment later. She pressed a small, two-way radio into my hand.

"I hid this, and the base station that goes with it, the night before the slavers trapped us. I just ... had a feeling. I didn't want them to find these things. The batteries are fresh and should be good for a few weeks."

I tucked the radio into my pack and gave the woman a nod of thanks.

"I'll call when I find work."

"See that you do."

Out of nowhere, she pressed forward and kissed me.

Startled, I asked, "What was that for?"

"You looked like you could use it. God knows I could."

Her eyes darted away from me, then darted back. "I want to see you again, Jake, but I've been through some things. I'm going to need time."

"I understand."

I did. Hers had been one of the screams I'd heard the night before my attack on the slavers. Those wounds only heal with time, when they heal at all.

I had turned to leave when I felt her hand on my arm.

"I mean it, Jake. Don't you dare forget me."

Her eyes locked on mine and fixed me with their soft brown. I wasn't going to forget her. In that moment, I knew it. Long or short, I would remember her for the rest of my life.

Fox, Ranger, and I struck out to find the slavers' home base.

We had ugly work ahead, and I was looking forward to it.

The Texas/Oklahoma Border
Late September / Early October
Year Three of the Plague
The Slaver Stronghold

I finished my latest scan of the place that, by all accounts, had to be the slavers' home base, then put down my binoculars and rubbed at my eyes. Nothing made sense here. Even taking only half of what I had heard as true, and the rest as tall tales told by the slavers, this place should have been bustling. Instead, it looked like a ghost town.

The boys and I had arrived here two days ago and had spent time ever since then reconnoitering the stronghold. We had kept to a safe distance, thankful for the brush that provided concealment, and we had studied the place with a furious concentration. At the end of that time, all we had to show for our work was a puzzle whose pieces didn't fit.

The compound was barely a wide place in the road, a collection of ramshackle buildings of wood and brick along with what looked like a couple of cobbled-together barracks. Calling it a town would have been charitable. Some attempt at fortifications had been made, but those consisted mostly of a barbed wire fence strung along the compound's perimeter. The fence was punctuated by a handful of peculiar gaps. From our distance, we couldn't tell their purpose and couldn't even hazard a guess.

The only part of the compound that looked remotely secure was a penned area at the end of the road. The pen butted up against the back of the slaver compound, and inside were maybe two dozen re-animates milling around. I had no idea what the hell that was about, but in my book it was insane. It made as much sense as living next door to a ticking bomb.

A thin haze of smoke rose from part of the compound, but I couldn't tell if it came from a cooking fire or something else. I was stuck in a situation where I didn't have enough information to make a solid plan, or even a flimsy one. My hopes, to gather intelligence and make a move from there, were falling flat. Concealed surveillance had taken me only so far, and I'd hit the end of what I could accomplish that way.

What the hell was I going to do now, walk in and ask around? I shook my head at the notion. Yeah, that would be completely unhinged.

On the other hand...

The next morning, Fox, Ranger, and I walked into the slaver stronghold. We strode boldly through the front gate, daring any living soul to stop us.

As my grandfather once said, if you have to walk into hell, walk like you own the place.

We knew immediately why the stronghold had looked abandoned. It had been overrun. Someone had attacked this compound, and they'd done a professional job. The gaps in the barbed wire fencing were clean, blown by some kind of shoulder-mounted rocket, based on the look of them. Bullet holes riddled wooden structures and pocked brickwork. The work looked efficient, sharp.

Deadly.

A trail of dried blood led me to the center of the compound and the source of the smoke. Bodies, thrown into a pile, had been doused with something and set on fire. Thin smoke, charred corpses, and the smell of cooked meat told me everything I needed to know. I had found the slavers.

Now all I had to do was find whoever it was who did this to them. I needed answers if I wanted to avoid joining that pile of smoking corpses. I started looking through the buildings of the compound, hoping to find some clues.

I hit pay dirt in the second building where I looked.

I had stepped inside the brick structure, my eyes adjusting to the dim light, when I heard the scream of a full-grown man, followed by sobs and begging.

"Jesus, please don't shoot! I promise I won't hurt anybody anymore! I swear to God I won't! Please, just please let me go! Please!"

There was a pause in the begging, then, "You … you're not one of them?"

"One of who?"

"Who do you think, man!" He gestured to my clothing, the camouflage that had been a gift from a dead soldier a lifetime ago. "The people dressed like you, that's who! They came here and shot the place all to hell, then dragged everybody into that pile and lit them like a fucking bonfire. Didn't give us a chance to explain anything."

"Did anybody call for a parlay, or did they just barrel in with guns blazing?"

The man sulked. "Well, one guy came in and said something about the guests we were keeping and how we should let them all go, or some shit like that. We told him these were ours fair and square and nobody was gonna take them from us."

"I see. And what happened next?"

The man laughed, bitterly. "The sumbitch told us his people didn't want to take our guests; they just wanted them to be let go. Can you believe that shit? We laughed in his face over that. The guy had no idea how the world works these days, that's what we said. We told him that you were either on top or you were property and that's just how things were now."

The man went silent for a moment, "Then the guy said something real quiet. We all thought he was talking to himself, only he wasn't. He was talking to someone outside, giving them orders, I guess. Next thing we knew they hit us. They shot through the fence and ripped into us. Sumbitches never gave us a fucking chance."

"What about your guests? What happened to them?"

He laughed. "The sumbitches let 'em go, that's what happened! They just cut them loose and sent them on their way like it was nothing. Maybe someone was out there giving them some kind of directions, I don't know. After all our hard work, those assholes just walk in and turn everybody loose."

"And the undead in that pen out back? What's their story?"

"Them? Well, when we'd have a guest who didn't behave right, we'd throw them in the pen and take bets on how long they'd last." He chuckled. "Pretty good entertainment now that there's no TV."

I grunted a noncommittal comment through clenched teeth. After a couple of minutes, I felt calm enough to speak again.

"Are there any others like you still alive here?"

No, man, there's nobody. It's just me." He spat. "Bastards killed everyone else."

I turned to leave the building. The man followed me out. Fox and Ranger were waiting outside for me.

The man grinned when he saw Ranger. "Hey, neat dog!"

He reached out a hand. Ranger growled.

"Be careful. He doesn't like strangers."

"Oh," The man pulled his hand back. "So, what are you doing here?"

"Nothing much, it would appear. I'm just passing through." I surveyed the buildings around us and set my pack down on the road beside a short length of steel pipe, debris from one of the ruined buildings. I squatted beside the pack and made a show of adjusting the straps.

"Now, when you said, 'guests,' you meant 'slaves,' right?"

The man bristled. "That's a dangerous question, buddy. I'm not sure I like the sound of it."

I shrugged. "Pay it no mind. I just want to make sure I have everything straight."

"Well, it's like we told that other guy. Either you're on top or you're property. It's the way the world works now."

"No, no it isn't."

I reached down and gripped the pipe. I spun on my heel and slammed the length of steel against the man's kneecap. The crunch of shattering bone vibrated through the steel of the pipe and into the palm of my hand. I felt the man's leg giving way and watched him drop to the road, off balance and in obvious pain.

I stood up and took a flare and three sticks of dynamite from my pack. I checked the fuses, shortened a couple, and left the third fuse long. I tucked that stick of dynamite in my back pocket. Then I struck the flare to life and lit the fuses on the other two sticks.

The slaver remained on the ground, gripping his crippled leg and swearing at me.

"I'll be right back, so don't go anywhere." I tossed the dynamite into the last two structures within reach of the man, then ran with Fox and Ranger out of range of the coming explosions.

We ducked behind a building at the edge of the compound, then heard the crump of twin detonations. We took our time walking back to the slaver.

"What the hell was that for?" he screamed. "What the fuck are you doing?"

"Just some clean-up. I needed to make sure those buildings were closed up tight." I hefted my pack.

"What the fuck, man! Are you just going to leave me here all alone?"

"No, I wouldn't dream of it." I lit the fuse on the third stick of dynamite and threw it toward the pen holding the re-animates. It landed just short of the containment wall.

"When that goes off, you'll have plenty of company."

I squatted close to the man, but not too close.

"I left you with one good leg and plenty of open space. See how far you can crawl before they reach you. Maybe, if you're luckier than you deserve, you can get away."

The slaver was back to pleading. "But why are you doing this, man? I never hurt you! I never did anything to you!"

"You and your buddies hurt a lot of other people, and some of them were people I know. This is payback. This ends it."

The slaver was snarling again. "Do you think this makes you a fucking hero? Do you?"

"No, I'm just an exterminator, killing the last rat in the nest."

I started walking away. Fox and Ranger fell in beside me.

I heard the man shouting after me as we left the compound.

"You think you're a good guy? Is that it? Well, you're not a good guy! There's nothing good about you! You're the fucking devil! You hear me? *You're the devil*!"

We heard the distant thump of the last stick of dynamite going off, then we heard a familiar chorus of moaning. The re-animates were out of their pen and on the move.

The slaver's yelling continued until it turned to screaming.

Then the screaming turned to silence.

The boys and I began our long walk back into Colorado, while I tried very hard not to think about the slaver's last words.

I didn't have much success.

The Road Back to Colorado
October
Year Three of the Plague
Time with My Thoughts

"You hear me? You're the devil!"

I was thinking about those words, the last I had heard from a slaver I had left to die. Truthfully, I was thinking about them pretty much to the exclusion of any real attention to my surroundings. Thankfully, I had a couple of companions who were taking up the slack. Fox and Ranger were making up for my lack of attention with plenty of their own. The boys stayed alert while I stayed busy overthinking my actions.

We had crossed the border between Texas and Oklahoma and were heading back to Colorado. Our route would keep us to back roads and would give us time to reacclimatize to the higher elevations of that familiar state. The weather was turning cool enough for outdoor camping to be comfortable without bugs being a problem. It would be an easy hike to the area of Colorado Springs and the Cheyenne Mountain complex, and it would be in friendly weather.

Now, if only I could get rid of those decidedly unfriendly thoughts about what I had done.

Killing, even straight-up murder, had become familiar to me a long time ago. I had just recently dispatched a band of what could loosely be called men with the kind of compassion I would use to stomp a cockroach. They had been slavers, the lowest of the low, and as far as I was concerned, they had gotten what they deserved.

What made this case different? What was it that made the death of this last slaver a thing that bothered me?

I had found the man alone in what had been the slavers' stronghold, and I had listened to his story of the stronghold being attacked by an outside force. According to the slaver, the outsiders had sent an emissary who asked them to release the people they were keeping as slaves. The slaver told me they had refused to go along with the man's request and had even laughed in his face.

That had been their big mistake. With a few quiet words, the stranger called on his people. Moments later, the slavers found themselves on the losing end of a short but intense firefight. According to the lone survivor, they never had a chance. I believed him.

Everything the man had told me, and all the evidence I could find in the slaver compound, indicated that the attack had been meticulous and professional. The bullet casings I found on the scene were hard evidence that the outsiders had used military-grade hardware. I had the gut feeling this was the work of Ranger's people.

Under any other circumstances, I would have felt better about that. I had been hoping to find signs that Ranger's people were still active, maybe still in the general area of where I had found him. Now I had evidence that both could be the case. That should have made me feel pretty good about the chances of finding these people, finding a place where civilization was being rebuilt, or at least where the undead were being held at arm's length.

The trouble was I didn't have room enough in my head to think about all of that, or any of it. I only had room to question what I had done. And what I had done had been pretty damn ugly.

After listening to the story of the surviving slaver, I had taken a length of steel pipe and crushed his kneecap with it. I'd then used two of my last sticks of dynamite to destroy a pair of buildings and deprive the man of any shelter. Then I had used my last stick of dynamite to blast open a pen where the slavers had corralled a couple dozen re-animates. The man hadn't been expecting any of this. I had taken him completely by surprise.

I had left the wounded man to try to crawl away from the re-animates if he could. Instead, he had chosen to spend perhaps his last minutes of life yelling after me. His demands and curses had done nothing except draw him to the attention of the undead. Chances are they had converged on him in that steady, unrelenting manner that was chillingly common to them.

The slaver might be dead now, or he might be one of the creatures he and his kind had kept for entertainment. I didn't care, either way.

I only cared about the way I had dispatched him.

What I had done went beyond cruelty. There was no getting around that. Murder was one thing. This was something else, maybe something monstrous.

And we all know that those who would fight monsters should take care, lest they look in the mirror one day and see a monster looking back.

Why then? Could I answer that nagging question? Why cripple the man and leave him to the mercy of the mindless when I could have accomplished the same ends by cutting his throat? Why this elaborate work when simple murder would have been more efficient? What was the reason, the motivation? What was the end to this means?

What was I turning into?

Was I becoming the thing I had fought? Was I becoming a monster?

Or was there something else driving me here?

The thought stirred from the back of my mind, crept out of the shadows where it had been hiding, and dared me to look at it eye-to-eye. Oh, there was something else at work here. I could deny it all I wanted to, but it still wouldn't go away. I knew that. I knew exactly why I did what I did.

The thought whispered, "*Face it, Jake. You were thinking of a pair of deep brown eyes and a voice that was soft with hope yet broken with hurt. And all you could think of was finding the people who had hurt her, and hurting them back as hard as you could.*

"*You wanted to find the people responsible for her suffering and pay them back for it. Isn't that what you called it when you hit the slaver? When you took a pipe, smashed his kneecap, and left him in the hands of death or something worse? Isn't that what you said? Payback? Weren't those your words?*"

And that was it, out in plain sight. There had been twenty slaves I had managed to get free, and God knows all of them had suffered to one degree or another. Simple murder of the last slaver would have been enough to ensure everyone's safety.

Or it would have been enough for nineteen of those people, but not all twenty. There had been one more, the one whose suffering had made a difference to me, and whose suffering had made a difference in the way I dealt with the last slaver.

So, Jake, maybe you're not the devil after all?

Maybe it wasn't about being a sadist or a monster or something even worse than either of the two. Maybe it all came down to paying back pain with pain and harm with harm. Maybe it was about making a statement: "You hurt *her*, and for that I will destroy you." That didn't excuse what I had done to the slaver, but at least that explained it.

The questions that had been nagging me finally had their answers, and the accusations that had been haunting me finally had been exorcised. The demons had fled back to their outer darkness.

Naturally, that left a nice vacant place for a horde of new demons to flutter in and take roost, looking at me from the shadows with soft, brown eyes. Something inside me sighed and shook its head.

I began setting up the evening's camp and getting out everyone's dinner.

"Well, boys, it looks like life can never be simple. There's always gotta be a complication. But this one, this one could be different. I mean, maybe there's something here, with her. Who can say, eh, guys? It's a slim chance, but still a chance. What do you think, boys?"

Ranger, ever the ally, thumped his tail and woofed softly. Fox groomed his nails, choosing to defer comment until after dinner was served.

We were well on our way to the Cheyenne Mountain complex and possibly finding Ranger's people.

After that, who knew what might happen or where the road might lead?

I fell asleep thinking of brown eyes and the last words I'd heard from their owner.

"Don't you dare forget me."

Colorado
Evening Camp, and an Early Warning

The boys and I crossed back into Colorado today, moving over that invisible line that marks the boundaries between states. According to my map, Oklahoma was now behind us, and our destination was waiting ahead. In an earlier time, I could measure the distance between the border and Colorado Springs in terms of a handful of hours. Now, on foot, I calculate it may take a couple of weeks, if not more.

Back roads and extreme caution accounted for the snail's pace of our progress. That and the fact that most of our trip through Oklahoma, down into Texas, and back up into southeastern Colorado has been across plains and grasslands. Open spaces can be beautiful, but if you're moving through hostile territory, they just make you itch between your shoulder blades. You never shake the feeling that someone, or something, is watching you. That's how it has been with us.

We'd had only the occasional sparse clump of forest or wooded area for shelter. Rarer still were the clusters of abandoned structures that were once the storefronts of small businesses. In some places we'd seen signs of struggles, firefights against the re-animates. In others, no signs of the living or the undead. In rare instances, we had discovered the remains of violent actions, bloodbaths of living against living.

The campgrounds we'd come across were the most disturbing sights. They had the air of places violently abandoned. It's as though people, in some sort of mass rage, had torn into each other before the re-animates could so much as lay a finger on them. If I had to guess, I'd say that people kept crowding into these places until the populations reached a saturation point. With people packed elbow to elbow, nerves strung tight, even the smallest incident could create an explosive release of tempers.

We never found any survivors of any of this violence. But the signs of struggles and frenzied fights long past were enough to make us take things exceptionally slowly and carefully. This journey has risks enough without me amplifying them by rushing to my goal.

We reached the southeastern border of Colorado late in the afternoon, maybe a couple of hours before sunset, tagging along in the company of a small stream that led us to a sheltered area with a clear view in front of us. It struck me as a good place to make camp for the evening and top off our water supply. It also looked like a good place to give me and my clothing a good soaking. The stream was cold, but cold water would clean me just as well as hot water. I had already set the evening's campfire, and I knew from experience that there would be enough heat to dry my clothes and get me plenty warm. I hung my clothes up to dry and finished setting up the tent while Fox and Ranger trotted down to the stream to drink their fill.

I'd made it a habit, since my earliest days on the road, to make sure I was never more than the walk of a day, two at most, from a supply of fresh water. In a world where nothing was certain anymore, it made me feel a little more secure knowing I could rely on at least one thing. Water was life, and it was the luxury of an occasional bath. On warm days, I could fill the bag of my portable camp shower from a stream, hang it in the sun for a few hours, and enjoy the nearly hedonistic pleasure of a hot shower.

Rivers, creeks, and streams had become good friends over time, and I had grown to know the language of the waterways. I knew the chuckling of brooks, the low mumble of rivers, and the hiss of water racing toward rapids or a fall. These waterways, once considered nothing more than items to note in passing, had taken the shape of friendly companions ... almost living things in their own right.

Camping came with more chores than checking water supplies and the state of my clothing. Since Fox and Ranger had joined me, we had assumed the occasional ritual of checking for ticks, fleas, and other parasites. I checked both of the boys, finding nothing. Truthfully, I would have been surprised if a flea or tick had turned up. Both of the boys had been free of parasites when I first encountered them, and they had stayed that way. The same held true of me and my gear. Things got dirty, but never got infested.

I could not understand why, but it tracked with so much else that I'd observed. The corpses I had seen in my travels had suffered from obvious signs of weathering, but little if any signs of decay. It was as if the Argus/Jones virus had hit the 'pause' button on every other pathogen out there. I was damned if I could figure out why or how, but I was glad it made it easier for us to stay healthy.

Next on the afternoon's agenda came a chore that Ranger loved and Fox hated with a passion. It was time for grooming. In addition to the clippers I used to keep my hair and beard from growing too wild, I'd picked up a couple of brushes for the boys. Ranger all but raced up to me when he saw them, while Fox hung back and dared me to approach. I gave Ranger a thorough brushing, in which he was a cheerful participant, and I complimented him on the state of his fur. He looked positively bursting with pride.

Then we both turned to look at Fox, who was glaring daggers at each of us in turn.

It can be challenging enough to brush a cat as it is. When that cat is roughly twenty-five pounds of muscle, claws, fangs, and gristle, 'challenging' morphs into 'damn near impossible.' It took a determined combination of tact, diplomacy and extravagant bribery to lure Fox into brushing range. Put another way, I opened a can of tuna and brushed Fox while he was busy decimating the can's contents. Fox paused from his eating to give me the occasional growl, promising feline retribution for my actions, but I was able to finish the brushing before he finished the tuna, so we agreed to be friends again.

I finished the evening's ritual by giving my hair and beard a trim, checking my look in a metal camping mirror. My face looked a touch thinner than it did when I started this journey, and some gray hair appeared at my temples and in my beard. I suppose I shouldn't have been surprised, but something I'll call vanity had reared its head lately. I had become a bit more conscious of my appearance. I had a feeling that had more to do with a past meeting with a singular woman than a potential meeting with Ranger's people.

The boys and I settled down to our evening meal. Counting the can of tuna, this made it two meals for Fox, but Ranger and I kept a pact of silence on the matter. I felt it wiser not to bring up the subject of cats and food, and Ranger was perfectly happy to finish his kibble and bask by the campfire.

I made sure to bury the leavings from dinner, along with my hair clippings and the boys' collected fur, in a hole by the campfire. When we broke camp tomorrow, I'd make sure to cover everything and leave no trace of our stay here. Even this close to our goal, I didn't want to leave anything for any unsavory sorts to find. I wasn't expecting trouble from any re-animates who might stumble across the remains of a camp. They were mindless things, This was a precaution against the living.

After mealtime, I set the wire and tin cans of our perimeter alarms and we all turned in to get a night's sleep.

I was jarred awake by the sound of metal cans clanking together, the low growling of a dog, and the chilling familiarity of a low whistling moan.

I bolted from my tent, bow and arrows in my hands and ready, with Fox and Ranger at my heels. We listened, senses sharp, for the shuffling of feet or the moaning that had broken our sleep. A re-animate was out there. It had crossed a trip wire and triggered the camp's alarm, and we had heard the thing moaning. Now, it had gone silent.

Where the hell was it?

The campfire had burned down to embers, so my night vision was keen. I nocked an arrow, listened for sounds, and looked for patterns of motion in the dark. Beyond the limit of the fire, we heard the low moaning starting up again, and Ranger jumped at the sound, tearing off toward the source. Fox ran after him.

I lowered my bow and waited for the boys to herd the thing in my direction.

There was the snap of a twig behind me.

I turned, hard. Less than a foot away from me, milk-white eyes reflected dull red from the light of the campfire's embers. A torn and rotted mouth opened to a low whistling dirge. A half-seen figure lurched forward, arms and open jaws reaching for me.

My arrow shot through one of those milky eyes and out the back of the thing's skull. The range was so close that I could see a glimmer of night through the hole my arrow left in the cranium. I could only hope that the arrow had done enough damage on the way out to neutralize the re-animate. I waited, holding my breath. The thing paused in the middle of a shuffling step, then slowly crumpled to the ground, folding in on itself.

Far away, I heard hissing and a low, growling bark. Then I heard a moaning followed by the splash of something heavy hitting a body of water. Something had fallen into our local stream, or it had been pushed. Either way, it was no longer a threat, and I was okay with that.

Ranger trotted up to the camp, followed closely by Fox. The dog had something in his jaws, something that looked like a tree limb at first. It turned out to be a desiccated arm. Ranger dropped the trophy onto the embers of our fire, and the leathery appendage flared up and burned its way to nothing but bone.

Good boy, Ranger. Good dog. Fox, I don't know what your part was in this, but good for you, too.

I pushed the remaining re-animate into the embers and watched as it caught fire and burned like paper. Only bones were left. I observed carefully as the thing was consumed. It had taken so little heat to set the thing ablaze, and it had burned with an alarming ease and speed. That was handy knowledge to have, and I suspected I might need it sooner rather than later.

After months of almost no contact with the undead, I had dealt with two of them in one night. That was a disturbing increase, and I had a nasty feeling that it was only the beginning. Something walked up my spine and whispered that the living weren't going to be a problem but the dead would be. Oh, yes, the dead would be a serious problem, indeed.

I looked around the camp and decided there was no need to cover up and hide anything, not anymore.

"Well, boys, it looks like we may have some company out there. Best we keep a sharp watch for trouble from now on."

I packed up and gathered our supplies. Dawn was breaking as we set out deeper into Colorado.

I knew that, between us and Colorado Springs, the undead were waiting. I'd have given real money to know how many.

Colorado

October

Year Three of the Plague

The Haunted Forest

Our journey has now taken us further into Colorado, and deeper into a disturbing change in the feel of things. The sky seems darker, an omen of another October and another year where the skin of the world crawls with the undead. It is though the sun has grown weary and dimmed its light. There is a sense of menace that hangs everywhere with an unearthly patience. Something that does not breathe is holding its breath, and it is waiting for us to take one step too many into a place from which there is neither retreat nor return.

There has been no sound here; no animals, no birdsong, nothing. Even the brooks and streams have been speaking with hushed voices, as if they are afraid of attracting the attention of things too unnatural to contemplate. I'd write this off to imagination if it weren't for the boys. Fox and Ranger have been exceptionally quiet, and their steps through this place have been light and deliberate. I've found myself copying their actions, with every motion the result of iron-clad intent. We've been moving through forested foothills, taking back roads through haunted woods, listening for any sound that is out of place, any sign of motion that does not belong in the world of living things.

I've been scanning the trees by the roadside in a habit born of a discovery back in my travels through the Gulf States. I had discovered a cluster of re-animates which had blended into a forested area, waiting so patiently that vines had grown up around them. I had only become aware of them when the trees had moved on a windless day. From that moment on, I respected and feared the patience of the undead. Today is no different for me.

My gaze today passed over old growth and new and came to rest on a skeletal face gazing with vacant eye sockets from the bole of a small tree. I stopped, and the boys stopped with me, all of us staring at that apparition. It never moved, never changed the angle of its face. It remained as still as a thing carved from stone.

I motioned to the boys to stay where they were while I nocked an arrow and moved closer to the thing. Its absolute stillness unnerved me, but also summoned my curiosity. I found myself driven to know more about this thing, even as I remained aware that it remained lethal; a bullet fired from a hand long dead.

I reached the tree and let my grip on my bow relax. The thing in front of me was long past any chance of causing harm. The skull face of the apparition had become a thing now of bark and bone, melding into wood. The re-animate had stood in place, with the infinite patience of its kind, unaware that there are things more patient still.

A small tree had grown in the spot where the re-animate stood so long and patiently. The small tree, seeking more nourishment than the soil could afford, took food from the minerals and rare chemistry of the nearest thing to it, the re-animate. It has now virtually entombed the thing and is consuming it over the long haul of years.

I looked beyond this sapling and saw the same scene played out perhaps twenty or more times. Re-animates, in various states of decay, had been imprisoned by growing trees. In each case, the undead was paralyzed, trapped by a tangle of roots and the shaft of a trunk that slowly grows and envelops the thing.

Some of the re-animates, a handful, tried to move their arms, but the movements were feeble. The trees now hold these things captive and are slowly drawing away the minerals that gave them motion and the semblance of life. The trees have already overtaken lungs and larynx, so that the undead have been robbed of even their low whistling moans. In time, even the bones will be gone. There will be nothing here but the trees.

I walked back to Fox and Ranger, my mood subdued and thoughtful.

Trees have resumed their march across the blank spaces of the world, bringing new growth and new forestation to places once abandoned to the mechanized hum of progress. In their return, they have captured and rendered powerless untold numbers of the undead. Probing shoots and green tendrils have pierced brain cases and dined on the decayed material inside, obliterating Argus/Jones in the process.

As I write these words, I find myself humbled by the day's discovery.

We have seen the re-animates exhibit a patience measured in years, yet we have seen how that patience can be their undoing.

The undead face nature, an adversary with a patience measured in eons, in the age of Earth itself.

Outskirts of Wiley, Colorado
Year Three of the Plague
The Territory of the Undead

The boys and I have begun a looping track toward our destination of Colorado Springs. I justify this path by telling myself that it's the best way to avoid the Interstate, large population centers, and potential infestations of re-animates. If we can keep to this route, we should be able to reach Cheyenne Wells in the next few days, then turn west and get to the Cheyenne Mountain complex. I'm optimistic that we'll find Ranger's people and a semblance of civilization, knock on wood.

The Rockies are a jagged gray line to the west of us, looking left. At least, I believe those are the Rockies. For all my experience, they may be foothills. Florida is not exactly famous for its tall, majestic mountain ranges. Beaches and theme parks tend to be our claim to fame. Hell, anything taller than a sand dune would qualify as a hill, based on my personal experience. To be honest, I could have been looking at the Rockies for days and not have known it. I spent my life in a state about as flat as a pool table, so I might not be able to recognize a mountain range even as I'm climbing it. Therefore, I remain thankful for paper maps to bolster my limited knowledge of geography. I can look at my position and the symbols and lettering for landmarks, and take the map's word for it all.

Either way, the boys and I are getting near our journey's end. Discovery, either of some shape of civilization or more ruins, is maybe a couple of weeks away.

All we have to do is get through God knows how many of the undead first.

Yeah, they've been increasing in number.

I'm not sure why we started seeing more re-animates now. The boys and I had spent months without laying eyes on a one of them. I've been wondering if this increase in sightings has to do with the fact that, relatively speaking, we're skirting closer to areas that were once more densely populated. It's a slight change from earlier patterns of travel, but it might be enough to make a difference. That would help explain why it feels like more of these things are coming out of the woodwork.

Thankfully, the rise in sightings of re-animates hasn't brought an increase in confrontations. We've largely managed to keep a safe distance from the re-animates. On those occasions where we've had no choice but to stand and fight, we've been able to deal with the undead easily. We've met them only in small numbers, and I've used my arrows to good effect while either Fox or Ranger provided a distraction. The encounters, though few and far between, have served to keep us sharp.

We've been traveling with caution during the day and ringing our camp with trip wires and alarms at night. I've been using the same gear that I've used since I began spending nights camping out in the open. It still serves me well. The only real change I've made is to keep a campfire burning at night. The undead, not bound by sight, have a chilling advantage when night falls. These little fires give me great comfort.

I'm not worried that our nightly fires might attract any criminal sorts among the living, even though that was a legitimate concern as recently as a couple of weeks ago. Now, if any living thing is out there, it will have to pass through the undead, who remain alert and invisible in the night. No, the boys and I are safe, alone within our small islands of light.

None of this, neither precautions nor reassurances, has made it any easier to sleep. I can still find myself jolted awake at odd hours of the night by the least sound. Sometimes all it takes is a stray breeze ruffling the fabric of the tent.

Daybreak here has been bringing a slow and sleepy start to more traveling, thanks to the residue of nights where sleep is fitful and easily disturbed. The scenery, though, can energize me quickly enough. God, but it is beautiful here. The views, the sense of the immensity of it all, it is all so staggering. Subtract the undead from the equation and add a pot of coffee and it would be a perfect place.

But the sense of foreboding and the absence of decent sleep have been conspiring to make our progress slow, and to make me more easily distracted. I've been feeling myself reaching inside, calling up reserves of energy to power me through one day to the next. It's a situation that can't last forever. I'm going to need some decent sleep and I'm going to need it soon. Soon, however, is not today.

Once again, the boys and I have broken camp and are continuing our trek north toward Cheyenne Wells and, after a left turn in that area, the destination of Colorado Springs. The mountains begin to rise on our left, soon to be obscured by the occasional woods.

And, everywhere, there is the sense that we are being watched by sightless eyes.

Colorado, Between Eads and Chivington

Rest, and a Break in Radio Silence

We pitched our camp today and chose a pleasant and secure locale to take a few days break from travel. The good news is we found a safe place with approaches we could easily watch during the day and guard with our perimeter alarms during the night. The bad news is we had no choice but to stop and take a break. Too many days in the open, with my nerves stretched like violin strings, had taken their toll on me. I was getting punchy.

I knew I was in trouble when I started seeing re-animates in every shadow. It's one thing to be alert and keyed up. It's another thing to see things that aren't there. Of course, the other side of that coin is the risk of not seeing things that sure as hell *are* there. That kind of exhaustion creates the perfect "Heads you lose, tails they win" kind of coin toss.

My exhaustion had caused me to lose a half dozen of my arrows, thanks to the fact that I was shooting at shadows. Usually, I retrieve my ammo and reuse it. In these cases, the arrows had been sent into shadows so deep that there was no way for me to know where to look. A couple of times, I had staggered on before I realized that I hadn't even tried to look for the spent arrows.

Staggering, by the way, is a perfect word to describe my progress. You can add the words "stumbling" and "sleepwalking" for seasoning if you like. The bottom line is I had worn myself down to a nub. If I didn't find time to rest and recharge, my body would pull the rug out from under me whether I liked it or not. The only sane course of action was to find a place to rest while I could still do it on my terms.

Thank providence for the rare smart decisions I can make. The boys and I set up our camp and, between us, slept for a solid day. On day two, we managed to stir ourselves and get some food inside us, but we did that between some long and welcome naps.

Sleep, peaceful and undisturbed, does not get nearly the credit it deserves. The body winds down and begins the long work of repairing itself from all the many exertions; all the "thousand natural shocks the flesh is heir to," as dear old Will Shakespeare would remind us. On the far side of sleep, we find ourselves alert and refreshed, and if not refreshed, at least ready and able to face that which may challenge us.

So it was, on day three, that the boys and I felt better than we had in a long time. My aim with the bow was back up to its old standards, as the pockmarks on a couple of trees and wooden signs could attest. My arrows were going where I sent them, and I was recovering every last one. Fox and Ranger were back to conducting practice hunting, sharpening their skills as predator and guardian respectively.

We also managed some old-fashioned play time together, and that was a balm for all of us. Ranger and I took turns with some play hunting and tug-of-war with some of my older and worn rope. Fox stayed aloof and above all that sort of nonsense, or at least he pretended to do that while Ranger was watching. When the dog's attention was diverted, Fox dove on the rope like it was a mortal enemy. We needed the play time as much as we had needed the sleep.

On day four I took a deep breath and decided on something I'd been putting off for a while. I'd been stalling for a number of reasons that, on modest inspection, looked pretty damn flimsy. I figured I could either keep stalling, or I could pick up the small radio in my possession and use it. I could make a call and see if anyone was on the other end to answer.

Fox, Ranger, and I had helped a group of people escape from a gang of slavers a few weeks ago. I'd given the former captives directions to my last winter camp. Their leader had given me a portable radio and instructions to stay in touch. There had been something in the way she had spoken those instructions that made me want to follow them. I had gotten to know the woman, slightly, and had found my thoughts wandering to her on more than one occasion. I had no idea if she'd spared any thought to me, and I didn't want to hope. But I had promised to call when I could, and I was fresh out of excuses.

I fished the radio out of my pack and plugged the batteries into it. I stared at the device as the power and battery lights came on, indicating a full charge. Truthfully, I felt as nervous as a middle-schooler making his first call to a girl. I took a deep breath and pressed the "transmit" button.

"Um, hello. This is Jake here, um, calling CQ ... um, over."

A number of words describing that opening comment came to my mind immediately. "Articulate" was not one of them. I glanced over at Fox and Ranger.

"Well, boys, that was pathetic. Would it be asking too much for one of you to please shoot me before I embarrass myself further?"

Neither Fox nor Ranger appeared to express any interest in doing me in. From the radio, there was only the hiss of static. I was beginning to hope that nobody had heard me, and I could forget all this and put it behind me. I moved my thumb to the "off" switch.

The radio crackled, "Jake? Is that you? Is that really you?"

It was her voice and it sounded warm and hopeful, and dear God, it was music.

"Oh! Uh ... hi, Della! Uh, yeah, it's me. So, how has everybody been? Are you ... uh ... are you all okay?" Oh yeah, I was definitely the king of small talk today.

Della told me how the group had found my old winter camp and had set themselves up as a solid community. They had lights and power, thanks to the solar panels that lined the roof tops in the neighborhood. They had planted gardens and had become self-sustaining. They'd also taken the precaution of building fortifications and defenses. They'd even run an antenna wire from their base station into one of the tall trees, increasing the range of their radio. Everything was shaping up for them at long last, and they would not be taken off-guard again.

"It's actually very nice," she said. "So, are you still planning to go where you said you were? Because, if you've changed your mind ..." she let the sentence hang.

"No, I still intend to get to the Cheyenne Mountain complex. Besides, I'm not sure I'd be good company. I went down a pretty dark road, Della, and I don't think I'm all the way back."

The hiss of static was back, then, "A dark road? Tell me about it."

So I did. I told her about finding the home compound of the slavers, and about how I had left the last of them to fend for himself or die at the hands of the re-animates. And I went back even further. I told her about all of the living I had killed, the bandits and scavengers and even the zealots I had murdered in cold blood. I told her about every one of my self-accusations, and I made no excuses for what I had done.

I drew in my breath, hesitating, then, "If it matters, the slave-takers won't be able to hurt you anymore."

"It matters." A pause, "Jake, I know you think you've got blood on your hands, but you need to know none of it belongs to the innocent. Not one drop of it."

"... Thank you. I really want that to be true."

"Please believe me. It is. And when you and your boys have done what you've set out to do, when you've found what you need to find and learned what you need to learn, you come back here. You come home to me."

" ... I'll try."

"You'd better. Or I'll hunt your ass down."

"Yes, ma'am," I couldn't help but feel a smile edging into my voice.

We broke the connection. I switched off the radio and removed the batteries. They would better hold their charge if they weren't tied into the device, and the risk of corrosion would be virtually eliminated.

I was in a thoughtful mood as I put everything back into my pack, but I felt better than I had in a very long time. It wasn't just the rest. It was what the conversation had revealed.

Yes, I had killed, and I had killed in some ugly ways. I might kill again, too. I knew that. But I had never killed the innocent. Their blood was not on my hands, and never would be. Not if I could help it. Somehow, that knowledge took a burden off my shoulders. If such a thing as peace exists, perhaps I was a step closer to it.

I sat down beside Fox and Ranger, "Well, boys, you heard the lady. We'd better get through this alive or she'll skin the hide off of us."

We turned in for the night. I wanted us to be fully rested when we broke camp and continued our travels the next day.

The road ahead was growing shorter, but I had a strong feeling that we were not finished with the undead yet.

Colorado
Late October
Year Three of the Plague
And the Die Is Cast

The boys and I had been on the road for a little less than a day after my conversation with Della when I called a halt and pitched a temporary camp. I needed some time to think about that conversation and what it implied. I wasn't going to get that thinking done properly if I was on the road and on the lookout for re-animates. I needed to sit down somewhere, if only for a day, and do some hard thinking.

Della and her fellow travelers had turned my old winter camp into a thriving community, transforming it from the way station I had known. The place had become a home and she'd made it clear that I was welcome there. It was more than that, actually. Della had made it clear that I was welcome there with *her*, and I'd realized that there was 'home' and there was 'Della' and for the life of me I could no longer separate the two. Where she was, that would be home and all that was wrapped up in that warm little word.

Then, there was Colorado Springs and a journey I had begun, God, three years ago. It was the search for any remnant of a civilized and structured society and it had been given a greater sense of urgency by the discovery of Ranger and, later, the bullet-shattered remnants of a slaver compound. There was also the weight of eight dog tags in my backpack and the promise I had made to guardsmen long dead.

Finally, I could feel the breath of winter on my neck driving me in one direction or the other, but not both. Wherever I went, I would need to camp there for a long time, perhaps months. The weather was not going to let me make one decision and then change my mind after a couple of weeks. Whatever destination I chose, I would need to be there and be firmly ready for winter before the snows arrived. It was already going cold at night and taking longer to warm up during the day.

A time of choices had arrived. Like it or not, I had to make a decision soon and I had to stick to it. There wouldn't be any time for a do-over.

On the one hand, there was the idea of home and a person I was missing more by the day. On the other hand, there was duty and a promise I'd made long ago. There was also a faithful dog named Ranger and my promise to him that we would find his people if they were still there.

After a full day of wrestling with my conscience, I made my decision. It would be easy to go the community Della and her people had created. Lord, it would be so easy. But I knew that, if I went to her, a winter respite would turn to spring then summer and then another year. I would never keep my other promises. I would never be the person I wanted her to see when she looked into my eyes. That was the last and biggest in a string of arguments and counter-arguments.

Dedication to promises and devotion to a pair of soft brown eyes had cast the deciding votes and forged my decision.

I would continue my journey to Colorado Springs. If Ranger's people were still there, we would find them. I would keep my promises. When that was done and the winter had thawed to spring, then I could go to Della. Then I could go home.

I turned in for the night, ready to break camp and move on the next day.

Colorado
The Road to Kit Carson

The boys and I have resumed our travels through the plains of southeastern Colorado, and, for once, the open areas haven't made me feel like I'm exposed. The plains are punctuated by small clusters of woods which have turned out to be friendly places to camp at night. Fresh water is always close at hand. The landscape has been providing tantalizing hints at what waits ahead, giving undefined promises of hill country, high-altitude forests, and mountains that scrape the floor of the sky.

We intend to head north to just below Kit Carson with Cheyenne Wells as our beacon city to the northeast. When we get to the area just south of Kit Carson, we'll take the back roads west into the town of Karval in Lincoln County. From there, it's a little more time in the high plains and river valleys, then the easy slopes that lead to the mountains of Colorado Springs.

The boys and I are well-fed and well-provisioned, thanks to the owners of an old-fashioned general store. The store, just a stop in the road, was completely abandoned. Taped to the front door, a note had been written in marker on weathered cardboard. It read, "To any of the living who find this store: it has been good to us, so let us be good to you. Be welcome to take what you need but leave plenty for those who come after you. May you find a safe place in this dangerous world."

A sense of kindness hung about the store. The arrangement of shelves and open spaces, the positioning of countertops and seating areas, all seemed to speak of a time when people gathered here for the common social discussions involving everything from the pressing issues of the world to the matter of rain next Tuesday. Lives were shared in this place, perhaps shared across generations. Now, all that remained was a friendly vacancy, the offer to share, and the reminder to share with others.

There was no indication that anyone had been to this store before the boys and I showed up. Dust, in layers, lay undisturbed everywhere. Our footprints left clear tracks in the floor. They were the only signs of any passage through a sea of dusty gray.

We spent the better part of the week at the store, checking on supplies and, as the sign requested, taking only what we needed. We found canned goods and pet food along with some good heavy socks. I even found a decent first aid kit with gauze, a roll of tape, a stretch bandage, some cotton balls and iodine, and some antibiotic ointment that may or may not have retained its potency. I checked for sporting goods and camping supplies, finding plenty of gear like I already had, but no arrows to replenish my supply. I still had a couple dozen arrows left, but some of them were beginning to show their age. Maybe I'd find some in another store, somewhere farther up the road.

The day before we left, I went to work in the store with a broom and a handful of dust rags. I swept the floors and dusted every shelf I could reach. I didn't do it to hide evidence that I had been here. I'd given up on doing that a week or two back, once I'd realized I was likely the only living thing around. No, I did this because it just felt right. It was a way to show my appreciation to the owners of this store, and maybe leave it in tidy condition for them if they ever managed to return. It was the closest I could come to a Thank You note.

As a last gesture, I oiled the latch and hinges of the front door. It opened and closed smoothly now. I looked around the store one last time. The place looked a little lonelier for all that it had been cleaned up. Perhaps the act of cleaning had emphasized the fact that the shop's owners were gone and might never come back. I hoped that would not be the case. A part of me really wanted the generosity of these people to be repaid with their safe return and their return to the life they had known before this all-consuming plague.

"Well, boys, it was nice to visit this place, but I guess we have everything we need now. No sense delaying things. It's time for us to hit the road again."

I left the general store, Fox and Ranger walking in step beside me. The door softly clicked closed behind us.

I had a strange feeling as we moved on, like something shadowy and patient was following just behind me, waiting for something.

Lincoln County, Colorado
November
Year Three of the Plague
The Gauntlet

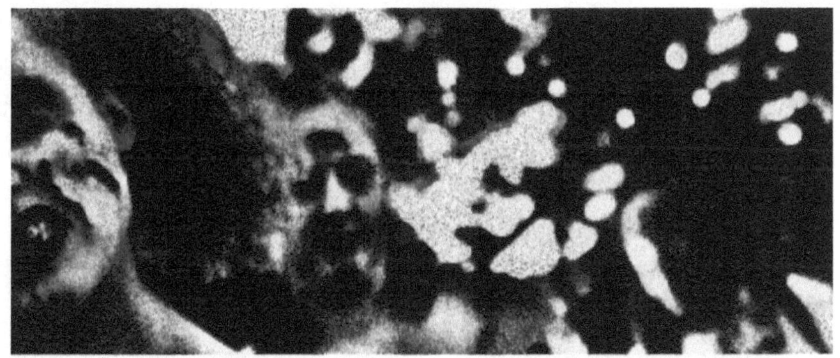

Their name was legion, for they were many.

We had just crossed the line from Cheyenne to Lincoln County when we ran across the re-animates, and I had never seen such numbers in one place. They didn't cover the land from horizon to horizon, but there were clumps and groups of them scattered about and too many to count.

Looking through my binoculars, I would see a small group of them staggering along the road ahead of us. Then, scanning to the right or left, I would spot another grouping not too far away. Sometimes they were walking, sometimes just milling around. Sometimes they were standing perfectly still with the infinite patience I had seen more than once. There was a vast crowd of them, and while they weren't a solid block to my path ahead, there was no place that was completely empty of them.

They ambled along the roads and in the grasses and wooded patches beside the roads, shuffling in the staggering, shambling way of the undead. Sightless eyes roamed the horizon, looking for God only knew what. Every so often, that low, piping moan issued from a desiccated throat, then the silence of their shuffling walk would resume.

The thing that bothered me, scared me if I'm to be honest, was the fact that the motions of these re-animates made them completely unpredictable. I could kill a group of them only to see more of the undead flow in to fill the vacant space, as water would fill a hole dug in the wet sands of a beach below high tide. Dig as much as you might want, the water would always return. It was the same thing here, just with walking corpses that were a damn sight more dangerous.

Just down the road was the town of Karval, and the chance to find a place to hole up and rest before making the final push to Colorado Springs. Between us and that town, however, there milled that ocean of the undead. If the boys and I were to reach our destination, we were going to have to get through them, with no opportunity to rest.

We had no choice. We had to run the gauntlet.

I kept my voice at a whisper. "Boys, stay with me. I'm going to let the arrows do the heavy lifting, so don't try any heroics."

In another time, I would have believed I was just talking to myself. Now, I had no doubt that Fox and Ranger understood my every word. I just hoped that they were in the mood to agree with me and not in the mood to decide they had better ideas. Because there weren't any.

I moved close to the first grouping of re-animates, nocked an arrow, and sighted on the undead that was farthest from the center of the group. I let the arrow fly, bringing down the first of what would be countless numbers among this legion.

I worked my killing spree methodically, dropping one re-animate at a time, until the entire group was lying motionless in the road. Then I recovered my arrows and moved either a few yards or maybe a hundred yards to the next group, where I started the process all over again.

The re-animates might be clustered relatively close, on the road or off to the side, but the groups weren't large ones. They were easy enough to handle, and I was able to recover and reuse my arrows after each group I dispatched.

The re-animates were never grouped more than a quarter of a mile away from each other. That meant I had no time to rest or to relax my guard. I had to keep alert and keep going, killing with all the precision and focus I could maintain. I could feel it wearing me down. Mind and muscle felt the toll this was taking on me, the slow but relentless drain.

I killed the re-animates one at a time, either as single members of a group or as solitary undead shuffling within the distance where they might take note of me and begin the moaning that would alert others. My aim remained steady, but it was taking longer to sight and loose an arrow for a killing shot.

I only had to look behind us to know that I didn't have any choice but to keep going forward. Re-animates milled and staggered along the road in the distance, filling the empty spaces left by the ones I had killed. Just as water fills that hole dug near the surf, they filled the places vacated by the undead I had dispatched. The boys and I traveled in a bubble, with re-animates in front of us, behind us, and to either side. It was a large bubble, to be sure, but it would only take a couple of moaning re-animates to make that bubble collapse and crush us. We pressed on.

The sun was barely risen when we began our fight through the clusters of re-animates, and it was now well on the way to the western horizon. The bad news was that I was getting tired, needing more time to aim, and needing to get closer to my targets. I had missed a couple of shots earlier and didn't have the arrows to spare. The good news was that the buildings of Karval were in sight, and we just had to fight our way through a group of maybe ten re-animates before we reached the town and a shot at safety.

Did I say it was good news? It was welcome beyond the measure of relief. That town was an oasis in a desert of the undead.

The sun was setting as we killed the last re-animates in the last group between us and the town proper. I retrieved my arrow and let out my breath. It had taken us the whole day, but we had made it through the undead. We had a short walk into Karval and a place to camp for the night. There were undead on the road behind us, but they were milling around and not showing us any interest at all. It had been a hard day, but it was almost over.

We reached the edge of Karval just after sunset, and everything went to hell.

The town was infested. Re-animates packed every street and probably every side street, jostling each other and crowding every inch of available space. We were far enough away to be outside of their notice, and that was a rare blessing. It was about the only blessing to be had. We were in twilight, and we'd be in full darkness before long. Our hopes of camping in a nice, safe building were shot.

The boys and I could circle around the town and move on, but there was no guarantee that the ranks of the undead would be any thinner on the far side of Karval. We'd also have to travel in darkness, the native element of the undead. To make matters worse, if that was possible, we were tired and hungry, worn down to the bone. It added up to a rotten situation and a hell of a risk, no matter how we looked at it.

The bottom line was, if we were going to walk around the limits of the town with all its undead, we would need to move in absolute silence. We'd be dead tired in the deepest part of the night, under conditions where the re-animates held every single advantage. That didn't take into account my unsteady aim and dwindling supply of arrows.

We couldn't go forward without triggering a death trap, and we couldn't go back the way we came without running into the re-animates already gathering in the empty places behind us. We couldn't stay where we were, either. Sooner or later a single re-animate or a group of them would stumble across us, and their moaning would call down every last one of them.

We needed a plan, even though we were too tired to think of one. It was one of those rare times I really wished I still smoked. I could have used a cigarette to help me pull a few thoughts together. Hell, it would be worth the risk of lighting a match. I absently patted my shirt pocket, muscle memory numbly reaching for a pack of matches or a lighter, some kind of fire.

Fire.

A thought blew through the cobwebs in my brain, reminding me of an incident only a week or two back. I remembered a campfire which had burned nearly to ash, and Ranger dropping the limb of a re-animate into the embers. I remembered how the limb and the corpse of another undead had caught almost instantly and burned down to the bones. In the span of a breath, every weary thought fell away with the crash of insight, and a brilliant idea flooded my mind.

There were hundreds of re-animates crowding the streets of the town. They could burn so easily. All it would take would be a bit of fire delivered to them. And I had just the thing.

I dug into my pack and got out my fire-making tools. Then I took out the first aid kit I'd found at the general store. The bandages weren't any good, but there was that elastic stretch bandage and there were plenty of cotton balls. I could cut a little of the stretch bandage and wrap it around the shaft of an arrow, then tuck a couple of cotton balls inside and secure the whole thing with two band aids. My makeshift bombs would be easy to make but hard to burn on their own.

My packages would need encouragement if they were going to catch fire and keep on burning. They'd need something to help create a wicking effect. Yes, something like a candle or a small torch. That would do it. I had the means at hand. It was the antibiotic ointment, which had separated into its petroleum base. I got busy striking a fire and preparing a handful of arrows.

I was careful as I wrapped the arrows, putting the payloads just behind the arrowheads and making sure that the greasy coating was thin but thorough. The firelight, dim as it was, helped illuminate my progress. It also had the unfortunate side-effect of showing how close the undead were to our small pocket of safety. I exercised all the caution of a person who knew they were running desperately short on time.

I had nineteen arrows left, and enough ointment to turn four of them into burning missiles. After that, I would be out of petroleum and out of luck. I only needed one of my flaming arrows to reach its target, though. All I had to do was fire accurately, in the dark, with no idea of the range.

Yeah. Piece of cake.

Striking from this distance, in the dead of night, had been far from my first choice. I'd done everything I could to see how close I could get and make a sure shot. Every answer was the same: I could get close, but it would be too close. If I missed my first shot, the re-animates would be on me before I could draw my bow a second time. I would have to fire from the most distant effective range of my bow, and I would have to make it count.

I rubbed at my grainy eyes and did my best to channel Robin Hood.

I figured one arrow, maybe two, would miss completely before I knew the right way to aim. That left me two arrows to get it right. That was a damn thin margin of error.

I touched an arrow to the fire, let it catch, and drew back my bow.

The arrow arced through the night, coursing up before clattering to the street and burning itself out as the re-animates shuffled nearby.

Four.

I set another arrow, adjusted for the distance, and loosed the flaming missile. It bounced off the chest of a re-animate and skittered out of sight.

Three.

I knew where to send the arrows now, and knew my draw was just inside the range I needed. I'd have to pull as hard as I could to make the next arrow stick.

Light. Draw. Release.

Two.

The arrow hit the re-animate square in the chest and stuck there. Small flames began licking at the creature's shirt. I picked up the last of my prepared arrows and glanced down at Fox and Ranger. My voice was a whisper.

"What do you say, boys? One more, for luck?"

Draw. Release. And one for luck.

Bingo.

The arrow flew into the crowd and struck a re-animate in the belly. The creature stumbled back, tripped, and fell to the pavement, its leather flesh bursting. The fire took it instantly. We watched the thing thrash and fall still, its noise drawing other undead closer to it, closer to the circle of fire that defined the thing.

A low moan issued from a handful of throats, and we stared in amazement as more of the undead took up the call and began moving toward the burning creature. First one, then two, then more of the re-animates caught the fire that was moving like a contagion through their ranks. And still more of them started moaning and following the others toward the initial source of the sound.

The creatures could not feel the heat from the spreading fire. They only knew sound. A handful had been lured to that sound, mindless of the flames, and now the fire was spreading everywhere. The undead caught and burned like tissue paper, lighting the streets as they blazed up in their hundreds.

In minutes, the fire had spread to every re-animate in the town. The skies were bright with a brief, false dawn as hundreds of the undead burned. The boys and I looked on, scarcely daring to believe what we were seeing. The town was hardly touched, but everything inside it was ablaze.

One of the re-animates stumbled away, toward the outskirts of the town. It jarred into a small group of undead, leaving trails of sparks where it struck. The sparks grew into small, flickering flames which chewed into the undead.

And they continued calling each other with those low, whistling moans. Those who heard the moans staggered toward the others, and all of them shared the small cargoes of fire that spilled from one to another, leaving nothing behind but bones blackened with ash.

Our sanctuary grew from a bubble to an island, then a clear path to the town. The undead burned all around us, mindlessly spreading the lethal disease of fire among them. I had time enough to appreciate the irony of that situation before the boys and I headed into Karval.

We were all tired and I was staggering, barely able to keep on my feet as we entered the town. My initial burst of energy had at long last deserted me and I was looking forward to sleeping anywhere I could safely collapse. There was nothing in our path but heaps of dark, ash-colored bones. They clattered emptily as our feet kicked against them, the only sound in the empty town.

There was no other noise. There was no moaning and no dry shuffling of feet. All around us was nothing but a peaceful silence.

Dawn was breaking. Our long night was over.

We had beaten the odds. We had run the gauntlet and come out the other side. I could see the Rockies in the distance ahead of us. One final push would get us to Colorado Springs. But we were going to sleep first. We had earned it.

I found a small, single-story building that might have housed an office. It was empty and long deserted. I closed the door behind us and wedged a chair-back under the doorknob. Fox and Ranger curled up in a corner and I stretched out beside them.

I barely remember closing my eyes.

El Paso County, Colorado
November
Year Three of the Plague
The Final Push

The boys and I crossed out of Lincoln County with a clear road ahead of us. Karval and Lincoln County were behind us now, and so was a near-death experience with a gauntlet of re-animates. We had survived an experience that had brought me as close to death as I ever hope to get. Against all the odds, we had made it through hundreds, maybe thousands, of the undead.

Our spirits were high, and we were feeling tanned, rested, and ready as we drew ever closer to Colorado Springs. I figured we'd make one more stop, just to get any supplies we might need, then we'd be pressing on to the highway just north of Fountain.

I had decided that after this stop it would be safe to take the main roads. We would be close enough to Colorado Springs for the danger to be minimal, if there were any danger at all. I figured the roads would be clear, too, since we would be close to a number of military installations. My experience in Florida had taught me that the military took traffic management seriously. I was looking forward to getting to those roads, and was hoping we would, at long last, meet up with Ranger's people.

I scratched the dog behind an ear.

"Well, fellow, we might be finding your people soon. Are you excited about joining back up with them?"

Ranger surprised me. Instead of the usual thump of his tail, he looked up at me and whined a little. There was a doggy look of pleading in his eyes.

"Really, fellow? You still want to hang out with me and this reprobate?" I nodded toward Fox.

Thump, thump, thump.

"You hear that, Fox? Looks like we're going to be a proper crew."

Fox yawned, elaborately, feigning indifference.

I smiled to myself as I considered the curious shape this journey had taken over the course of these years. I had started alone, with only the slender hope that I might find something of civilization at the end of my travels, if I survived them at all. Then somewhere along the way I had found these two companions, and 'companions' was the best way to describe them. I couldn't imagine thinking of the boys in the context of animals. We had become more than what any of us might have been before the plague. We were fellow travelers in a wilderness, battle-tested veterans, and friends. If those two could talk and play poker, we'd be drinking buddies.

Then, there was the woman with her deep, brown eyes. Della had been completely unexpected. I wondered if we ever would have met, had we not met the way we did. She had changed me in ways subtle and profound, and there was no denying that. I had let her get closer to me than I'd let anyone since my ex-wife. Don't get me wrong. My divorce had been friendly enough, all those years back, but it had made me shy about any human connection. I had friends, but I kept them at a safe distance from me. I treated close human contact pretty much the way I'd treat something radioactive. Then, this woman had come into my world, and I wanted to be close to someone again.

I grinned sardonically. Well, I was back in the dating pool, and all it took was the collapse of civilization. A therapist would have a field day with that little gem, if there were any therapists still alive and taking appointments.

We were near the outskirts of Truckton and our pace was more of a leisurely stroll than it was a hike. It felt good to be taking it easy with the boys. There was no trouble to be seen in any direction, and we were close to a strip shopping center. I blessed the municipal planners and developers who had chosen to put commercial enclaves like these at just about any place in the country where two roads intersected. In the times before the plague, these stores could be a nuisance. Now, they were a lifeline.

This shopping center had a barbershop which appeared to be mostly intact. I'd checked it for any lingering re-animates, then went in and gave myself a trim. I'd also given the boys a good brushing. After this, we would check the local stores for anything we might need, and I meant *need*, before going on the final leg of our trip.

"Gentlemen, Colorado Springs is close now, and we are going to look like a million bucks when we get there."

I examined my face in the barbershop mirror. Okay, maybe 'a million bucks' was stretching things in my case. My hair had started to get shaggy, and my beard really needed a good close trim. It had been a while since Della had trimmed everything up enough so that I looked more like a rugged explorer and less like an ancient hermit. The face in the mirror was still presentable, but it was definitely on the road back to Hermit Town. That might have been despite my efforts to keep things trimmed, or it might have been because of them.

My looks were weathered, but not bad. I had gotten a bit wiry over the course of my travels, though I would never be accused of being a bodybuilder. I'd also collected a few decent scars, and that was all fine with me. The image in the mirror spoke of a person who was comfortable in the wilderness. Fair enough, and maybe generous, considering how my situation had progressed since those first days in Miami. Lord, but I had come a long way from that time when I first started laying items out on my bed, wondering what was a luxury, and what was essential to keeping me alive.

I got the clippers from my backpack and started the work of getting my hair and beard back in shape. The barbershop had plenty of items, but everything except for scissors and combs ran on electricity and, guess what? It had been a long time since the turbines had turned over in this neighborhood or any other. So, I made myself look neat while I grumbled about all the gray that had somehow snuck into my hair. The gray hair probably waited until I was distracted with the task of not getting dead, then made its move. Gray hair is sneaky like that. At any rate, that was the story I was going to tell in case anybody asked.

I trimmed and clipped while Fox and Ranger watched, perplexed. They were probably wondering why I went to all this effort when I could simply brush. After all, if that worked for them, it should work for me.

Naturally, the boys got their turn once I was finished. Ranger was first because he was the easier of the two to brush. By the time I was finished, he had a sleek coat that was all business. He looked like a professional dog at the peak of his game.

Fox was next, and he was still a bit of a challenge. I chalked that up to a feline stubbornness that probably dated back to the days of the pyramids. I was pretty sure that Fox felt it was his duty to be stubborn as a way of paying respect to his ancestors if nothing else. On the other hand, Fox came by his stubbornness naturally, which meant I had to bribe him into sitting still for his brushing. I got out a can of tuna, knowing full well that bribery was the only way to motivate my feline associate.

By the time I was finished, I had collected enough fur to build a new cat.

"Fox, where do you keep all that fur, buddy?"

Fox sighed as if to signal that there was no way I could understand the mysteries of a cat. In all fairness, he was probably right.

I packed everything up, and we went to scout the rest of the shopping center. Most of the stores were relatively untouched, though the convenience store and a local TV repair shop had been ransacked, stripped down to the bare walls. In the case of the convenience store, I could understand it. People would grab anything they could eat, drink, or smoke in the rush of getting panic supplies. But the TV repair shop? That was a mystery. I'd seen it before, but that didn't make it any easier to understand. Sure, that fifty-six inch TV was never going to be a better bargain, but good luck watching the Super Bowl when you don't have power, streaming services, or any teams left to play the game.

The other stores helped us in our quest to find the supplies we needed, though we didn't need much. We were in pretty good shape. All I needed was a first-aid kit to replace the one I'd used up at Karval, along with some non-perishable food items to top off the menus for all three of us. The pickings were easy, and it was the work of an afternoon to get everything in order.

We set up an overnight camp in an office at the back of a small tattoo studio and relaxed for the evening.

The next day would see us on the Road to Colorado Springs. If everything went well and I had done a good job with my math, we would be there before local sunset.

Truckton, Colorado
Bitten
Infection + One Hour

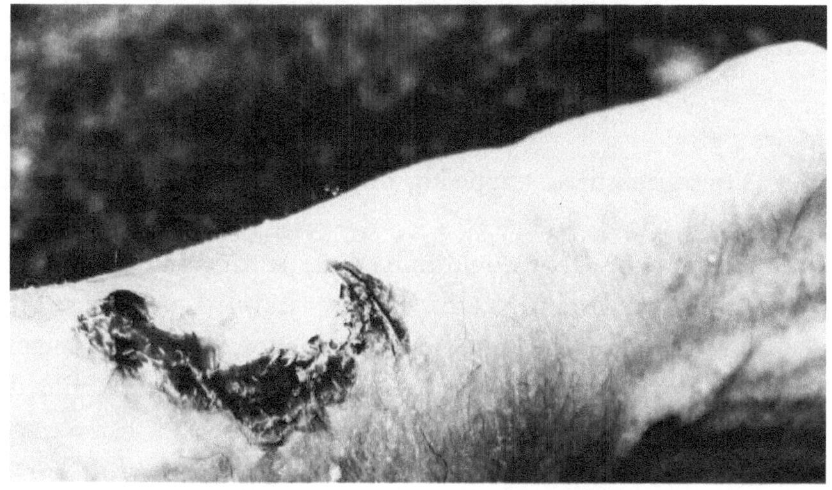

The wound was an almost complete semi-circle. It was an arc with long dashes between the smallest of gaps, where dark blood oozed in contrast with weathered skin. As semi-circles go, it looked to be a bit jagged, but still so very clear for a wound. It existed, yet still carried an air of the unreal.

The wound was on my arm, and I'd been staring at it for almost an hour, watching the thick blood rise and fill the gaps in my skin. In some ways, the wound was a masterpiece of biological devastation. It was a near-perfect puncture wound that came swiftly and sank deeply.

The curve of the wound started as evenly spaced dashes before the blood welled up to fill the spaces. The broken place in my arm was now the legacy of skin opened by the swift bite of rotting teeth. The initial spacing of the punctures mocked me as a grim parody of Morse code. I saw dots and dashes that repeated the same sentence over and over.

"You are going to die, foolish man."

I was going to die.

I found myself hypnotized by the injury. I watched with a grim fascination as the blood closed the gaps, filled the blank spaces, and slowly clotted. I let my thoughts be absorbed by the moment of the wound.

I was transfixed, trapped by my thoughts in the immediate ... in the 'now.'

And then? What would come next? What would happen when the curtain rings down on this life and rises on ... something else?

What will peer from gray and filmy eyes? What manner of thought or instinct will arc through the relic synapses of a mind dead and re-wired? What will drive my husk to rise and shamble across this world, another corpse that should be dead and buried?

These admittedly were grim thoughts, yet they may be among the last that I could call my own for all I can tell.

Lord, how did it come to this?

It was such a simple mistake, a simple stupid mistake.

We were leaving Truckton, ready for the final leg of our trip to Colorado Springs, when I heard a rustling sound coming from just around the corner of an abandoned building. Since that building was going to be behind me and to my left as the boys and I left town, I didn't want to leave anything to chance. A suspicious sound can lead to a nasty surprise for those too unwise to check it out ahead of time.

I moved to the corner of the building, bow drawn and ready, and turned sharply to face the source of the noise. It was nothing more than plastic sheeting being stirred by a breeze. I relaxed and let out a breath I didn't know I'd been holding.

I hadn't checked the near corner of the building for a doorway. Stupid, stupid, stupid man.

I had let my focus drift for perhaps a handful of seconds, and that was all it took. The thing struck like a snake, hitting before I had time to realize there had been a doorway or a thing waiting in its shadows, biding its time with an endless patience. And, in those instants, everything had changed for me. Everything was over.

I dispatched the thing that had killed me, driving an arrow into its skull with my bare hand. The re-animate collapsed without so much as a twitch, leaving me to deal with the last hours of my life. I had plans to make and carry out, and very little time to do the work.

I have since run the scene through my mind countless times, even though I've known there is no way to change what has happened to me.

All I've known for certain is that I had thirty-six hours left either before I turned ... or before I made sure that I didn't. That's thirty-six hours at the outside, and only if I'm lucky. It may be substantially less time than that, and I have already wasted an hour.

I hefted my pack and struck out for open ground, some place that's a safe distance from the buildings of Truckton.

I needed to get to a clear area so that I could settle things and give Fox and Ranger room to escape, or to fight the thing I could become. I knew how animals react to the undead, and I wanted the boys to have a clear path for a get-away or an attack.

My forearm was already beginning to feel cool as Argus/Jones seeped into the wound and began its relentless spread through my bloodstream. I moved quickly, not even bothering to bandage the injury.

Time was against me now.

Outside Truckton, Colorado
Infection + 12 Hours

I have chosen to start sending these journal entries in real time now, uploading everything as soon as I finish each day's chronicle. I'm going to apologize for that, but the immediacy of my situation demands that I don't wait for so much as a day to go by while I order my thoughts. I have to get this all on the record now. I can't afford second thoughts for a tomorrow that may not come.

I found a clear space and got to work on settling the last of my accounts earlier today. I haven't slept since being bitten yesterday, and I'm not inclined to rest now, not when I have no way of knowing how many hours are left to me. As a rule, a person infected by Argus/Jones has between twelve and thirty-six hours before the virus overtakes them, and I have just crossed the twelve-hour threshold.

I am working on borrowed time.

I set up my pack in essentially the same way a soldier in Florida's panhandle did a few years and a lifetime ago. That man was fiercely methodical, leaving packs full of supplies and a long note for those who might find his remains. I am following his example, with a few changes. I am putting my story, and his, in this journal and uploading it all to whoever might be around to read it.

I'm also working to describe my symptoms as Argus/Jones invades me and crashes through all the defensive barriers a human body can summon. It is strange to consider the fact that I may be detailing my own autopsy.

The wound on my forearm where I was bitten started out to be painful, but the pain soon faded to a sensation that was more of a chill. It was as though the site of the infection was cooler than the rest of my body, and that coolness was spreading. No fever at all, just that creeping sense of cold.

Now, the feeling is not so much a sense of cold as it is a sense of … distance. I feel like my body is slowly becoming less a part of me. I can move my limbs, but they are beginning to feel like they belong to someone else, and not me. My arms and legs all obey the commands of my mind, yet the commands seem to come from farther and farther away.

My movements have become more sluggish and disjointed, making it more difficult to carry out the work I need to do. It has been difficult, but not impossible. No, 'impossible' is coming, but it's not here yet.

Oddly enough, my mind still feels completely clear, despite the fact that I haven't slept.

Truthfully, I haven't felt a strong need for sleep. Fear and nervous energy have been keeping me going for now, along with the knowledge that I'll be getting an eternity of sleep before much longer.

I started a campfire this evening so I could enjoy a meal, maybe one of my last meals. Fox and Ranger have been sticking by me, though I can tell they know something is wrong. Before much longer, the boys will get skittish. But, at least for the duration of the night and the meal, I've had their company, and I appreciate it. There is a remarkable solace in spending my last hours with friends.

I will stay awake and finish my work. Maybe I'll have time to look around afterward and enjoy the scenery. It will be good to relax, however briefly, and enjoy my surroundings before facing the end that must come.

I have chosen that end. I won't force the boys to attack a thing that was once their friend. That's a level of cruelty that I refuse to contemplate. I can't spare myself, but I can spare them.

I have my pistol, and one bullet. I'd been saving them against a need like this, hoping that one day I would be able to put the weapon away, unused.

I guess that day isn't going to come, after all.

Outside Truckton, Colorado
Infection + 20 Hours

The sunrise was beautiful this morning.

I feel a sense of loss in writing those words.

It occurs to me that, with all I've been through, I'm not sure I've ever taken that handful of moments to appreciate something like this. Oh, I know the night and its stars very well; but the morning, the daybreak, their beauties have been strangers to me.

Only now, with the hours of my life slipping through my fingers, do I grasp those moments. I had an entire lifetime to take some sort of notice of all this, and I doubt I gave it much more than the occasional fleeting thought. Now comes the regret over missed opportunities.

The paradox would be laughable if it weren't so damn painful.

I stayed awake through the night. I needed to get my pack in order, securing precious equipment and information against the elements. I wanted the important stuff to be weatherproofed in case it might take longer than expected for someone to locate my remains. I did my work by firelight, enjoying the dance of the flames for what may be the last time.

I secured that set of dog tags from the soldiers I had found near Pensacola, and instructions to deliver them to any military officials who might be found. It had been my hope to deliver these, myself, once I had reached Colorado Springs. I had made a promise to the shades of those men that I would see their dog tags delivered and their story told. Since that was going to be out of my hands, the best I could do was write the information down and leave it.

I know someone will find what I'm leaving. I know who it will be. It will be one of the people I had helped to escape from a group of slavers.

So all my moments boiled down to just a handful of tasks and all those tasks, all the contents of my life, fit neatly into a backpack.

And then there was the one item I had been putting off, for a number of despairing reasons. It was a call I had to make, and it's one that I knew was going to hurt.

But, my hours weren't growing longer.

It was time to make that call.

I took my radio from my pack, put the batteries into it, and checked the charge level. A little better than half-full, more than enough for what I would need.

I thumbed the 'transmit' button.

"It's me, Jake, calling CQ. Anybody there? Over."

It only took a moment for someone to respond. It was an unfamiliar voice, but a friendly one.

"Hey! Good to hear you! Stay where you are, okay sir? She's nearby and she wants to talk to you. Let me go get her."

"Wait, I -" but it was too late. I was talking to the silence of a carrier wave. In a moment, that changed, and I was listening to a voice I had come to know fondly. And it broke my heart to hear it.

"Jake! Hello, you rascal! Have I got some news for you! But before I give you all the good gossip, have you found what you were looking for? Or have you called to say you're coming here?"

" ... I'm afraid the answer is no, to both. I'm sorry, Della, but there has been an obstacle. And it's a big one. I need to tell you a few things."

The voice paused, then continued, subdued, "I'm listening."

I explained what had happened. I told her everything.

For a few moments, there was silence, then, "No. No. Please, no."

"... I'm sorry."

The voice was choked, but determined. "What do you need me to do?"

"I need someone to get my backpack. If you could send someone, I've left instructions about what needs to be done with it. There are dog tags inside the pack, and I promised that they'd get to the right people."

"We can do that. Give me your coordinates if you have them, or just tell me where you are."

I gave her the information she needed, filling in both the Earth coordinates from my map and providing landmarks.

"But be careful. We had to fight our way through a few hundred re-animates to get here, and I'm pretty sure there are plenty more of them out there. Be very cautious."

"Don't worry. We've got all that under control. Is there anything else you need, Jake?"

"Yeah, there is something, something important," and my voice fought its way through a sudden tightness in my throat. "Della ... could you please take care of Fox and Ranger? I don't want the boys to be alone, and I ... I think they'd like to be with you. They'd appreciate having a home."

"I can do that. I can look after them for you."

"... Thank you."

"Is there anything else? Anything you need for ... after?"

"No, there's nothing. The people you send will know what to do. I'll make sure that any last instructions are clear. I hope that will be enough."

"... We'll make it work, so don't worry," There was another pause, as if she was thinking about her next words and measuring them carefully.

"Jake, there's something thing I need to tell you; something I had been hoping to tell you when we had the time." Her voice broke,

"But I guess time is something we don't have any more. I want you to know this, I *need* you to know this, no matter what hap-"

I broke the contact before she could finish.

I couldn't bear to hear what she was going to say.

Outside Truckton, Colorado
Infection + 32 Hours

It has been a struggle to write this. It's hard to frame the thoughts and it would be nice, so nice, to rest and sleep. I don't dare. Nothing that is me would wake up.

So I write now and send to you so you may read. Very sorry, but my thoughts are vague, balled in cotton. They come from far away.

The hole is roughly three feet wide, three feet deep, and six feet long. I call it a hole, even though I can't fool myself about what it really is. The people who find it, and find my remains next to it, they'll know well enough what to do. Digging it, I thought about a man I had never met, yet who managed to teach me through his own example.

He was that national guardsman whose last act I had encountered in Florida's panhandle. He and his companions had been exposed to contaminated blood. They had known what their ultimate ends would be, so they'd dealt with matters in their own way. I had found the last of the guardsmen sitting near the only open grave in a row of them, with a single bullet wound penetrating his brain case.

The guardsman had left a cache of supplies behind for anyone who could use them. It was all so precise and military-neat. He had also left behind everybody's dog tags, and I had carried them with me through my travels. I had hoped to give them to a proper custodian. Now I must pass this charge along, and hope that someone else will succeed where I failed.

God, I had come so close, so close. But this place, this open field, marks the limit of my travels. I can feel the infection strengthening its hold, digging ever deeper into me. I am nearly out of time.

My movements have become more sluggish and disjointed, and it is taking longer to do even the simplest things. It took me all night to dig this hole and it's taking most of the day to type these words. My thoughts get slower and harder to frame. It's all gotten so hard.

No fever, no pain, either. Just the sense of distance, the watching as something takes over my body and leaves less of it for me to control ... I lose a little more of myself with each minute.

Is it warm today? Cool? Is there fresh air in a breeze? I don't know. There is nothing left to feel. No smell or taste of the air. All gone.

And my eyes ... vision is cloudy, getting worse. I see the world through gray film. Only yesterday the sunrise was so clear, so beautiful. Was it yesterday? Can't really remember. But this morning, gray sticky light and the sun just a blur. The day is grainy and dim. The light is draining from eyes that won't need it before long, eyes that wouldn't understand the light even if they could see.

The hole is dug, the work is done. My pistol is beside me. Just one bullet in the magazine. All I need, really. Soon, the last work I have to do.

The boys are gone.

It was yesterday, I think. Fox hissed at me and headed through the field toward a patch of woods. He was low to the ground, ears back and tail down as he slunk away. Then he turned and made a peculiar howl. I'd heard stories about that sound but had never heard it myself. It was the sound that cats make for the dead.

Ranger followed Fox, whimpering and making the sad eyes dogs know how to make. He kept low, moving away with his tail tucked under him, pausing to look behind him from time to time. Then he, too, was gone.

I had watched the boys before I went back to my digging. Just wanted to make sure they got to a safe place. In a way, I'm glad they left when they did. It means I got to see them through clear eyes. Today? There would have been only the fog.

Boys, I am so sorry that I have to leave you this way. Please understand this is something I never wanted. I'd hoped that we would get to Cheyenne Mountain together. I had really wanted to finish this journey with all of us together, and it hurts that I can't. Oh, God, it hurts. It hurts more than anything I could imagine.

I am so sorry, boys.

But we all know what has happened to me, and we know what I have to do. I won't turn into something you have to hate and have to fight. I can keep that promise, boys. And I will.

And don't worry, boys. You won't be alone. Someone is coming, and they will take you to your new home. It will be a good home. You'll be happy there. I know this person, so I can promise that, too.

I will miss you, boys. You were good friends to me, and I know you'll be good friends to the person who'll take you to your new home. She's a good person. Better than I was, and she'll keep her promise.

Please don't be sad.

My hands are starting to shake, and it is harder to write. Harder to see the words and harder to type them. Not much time left for me, not much at all.

I have to use the gun before my hands won't let me pick it up.

I will upload this journal now, send it to any of you who can see it. Sorry I never got to meet you.

Sorry I never had more time with the boys, or with her. But I think she knows how I felt. I hope she does.

I have to go now.

I never thought it would end like this.

Outside Truckton, Colorado
Infection + Forty-Seven Hours
"... Lazarus, Come Forth"

Whipwhipwhipwhipwhipwhip

I remember that I felt really terrible. That was a problem, or at least a puzzle.

Whipwhipwhipwhip

I mean, I shouldn't have been feeling *anything*. Or remembering anything. Right? I didn't understand any of this.

Whipwhipwhip

What was going on? ... Made no sense, none of it ... And it was hard to think. No, I couldn't be thinking. The dead don't think.

Whip ... whip ... whip ...

And that sound. I *knew* that sound. I remembered it from somewhere. How? There it is again, the big puzzle. The dead don't remember. Or do we? Dear God, what if it's all wrong? What if we do remember? What if we think? What if we weren't what everyone has believed us to be?

Through it all, my head hurt. I felt terrible.

Whip. Whip. Whip.

I remembered that sound. From Miami. Helicopter blades, slowing down. And there were voices. Fuzzy and vague, but I heard them. I heard a man's voice, coming toward me.

"Sir? ...Hey, sir, can you understand me? Just give me a signal. Move your head if you can. Try to speak."

That voice ... very professional. I tried to focus my eyes. A man. In some kind of uniform. He ... he had a gun.

My thoughts, sluggish and painful, gave way to full panic. *Oh, Jesus, he has a gun and he's going to shoot me! No, no mister, I'm not like the other dead. I'm different! Dear God, say something to that man! Say something or he'll shoot you!*

I lifted my head. A moan escaped my lips. *No! God, no! Not good! Try again! Try again, damn you!*

"Not ... like ... other ... dead. Different. I swear! Not shoot! Please!"

"Sir, it's okay. Nobody is going to shoot you. You're not one of them. You're not dead. You're alive. It's kind of surprising, to be honest. We came here expecting to find a dead man."

" ... Alive? ... Me?"

"Yes, sir, you. You're alive."

"But ... I was bitten."

I showed the man my arm. He saw the wound but didn't react the way I thought he would. He nodded his head, but he didn't take any other action. He didn't back away, didn't raise his rifle, didn't do anything like that.

Instead, he asked me a question.

"How long ago were you bitten, sir?"

"I dunno ... a couple of days maybe?"

"A couple of days, or close to it. That sounds about right, based on what she told us. Way outside the time you would have turned into one of them if it was going to happen. Not a bad bit of math for someone in your condition."

"She? ... My ... condition?"

"Yes, sir. You look pretty beat up. Honestly, you look like hell, but yeah, definitely alive. You've got a nasty scalp wound, though. We should have it checked as soon as we can. Looks like it's still bleeding a little."

Bleeding? But the dead don't bleed. Maybe I *was* still alive? I pressed my hand to the side of my head. Pain seared a path through my brain and rocketed back from the far side of my skull. My stomach heaved. I vomited and passed out.

***

Grrrrr ...

  Grrrrr ...

My head hurt like hell and now Ranger had to start growling at something. Why did this all have to happen when I was trying not to be dead? Really not fair, not fair at all.

"Sir? Are you awake? Can you hear me?"

"Trying," I coughed and retched a little. "Trying. Really alive?"

"Yeah, you really are, sir, and I'd appreciate it if you would calm down your dog. He isn't letting us get close to you."

Grrrrr ...

"It's okay, Ranger. It's okay."

The growling stopped. The pounding in my head didn't.

"... Sir, did you say *Ranger*?"

"Yeah. He's a good dog."

"Sir? Did you name him that?"

"No, no. He ... came that way. Had tags. He was somebody's. He's a good dog."

The voice turned soft, "Well, I'll be damned. Yes, sir, he *is* a good dog, and we thought we'd never see him again."

Then, "Sir, you're not going to believe this, but we know that K-9. He was one of ours, part of our unit. The poor fellow lost his partner and we thought we'd lost him, too. I guess he found a new partner. You've got a really good companion there, sir."

"Yeah, he's a good friend. We look after each other."

"Um, I don't suppose you know the cat, do you? He's being pretty difficult, too."

The cat?

I heard another voice. "I know the cat. I can help with him."

I *knew* that voice. I jerked my head up to get a better look. That ... was a mistake. Pain exploded in my brain. I vomited violently, and the world went away again.

***

The world came back in pieces, taking its time. My brain gradually knitted itself back together. Slow going through the pain. Oh, boy, did my head hurt. My stomach was still churning but settling down. That was something, I guess.

Good lord, being alive is harder than I remember.

I was lying on my back, my head resting on something soft. I felt warm droplets of rain on my face. Rain drops, but they tasted like salt. That didn't make sense. I opened my eyes, tried to focus.

There was no more gray, but everything was still a little blurred. It took a moment, but a pair of brown eyes swam into view. I knew those eyes. And, tears?

Yes, tears. I could hear sniffling. *Don't cry. It's okay. Please don't cry.* I cast around the bruised and aching corners of my brain, trying to think of something reassuring to say.

"I barfed. A lot."

The salt rain still fell, but there was a laugh among the sniffles. A gentle hand stroked my hair, on the side of my head away from the pain.

"I know, baby. I saw it all. You were quite the mess."

"I thought I heard a helicopter. Did I?"

"Yes, yes you did. They found us a while ago. I was going to tell you when you called, but you hung up on me. They gave me a lift."

"That was very nice of them."

"Oh, I insisted." Her voice paused, then continued softly. "I'm glad we found you like this, and not like..."

I didn't say anything. I didn't need to. We all knew what she had expected to find.

The other voice came back, "Sir, we really should get you to a medic. Do you think you can stand?"

"I'll try," I wobbled to my feet. The world spun, my stomach twisted, and a bunch of really nasty elves hammered spikes into the side of my skull.

But I could stand.

I tried to smile, and that came out a little wobbly, too, "Okay. Now what's next?"

She leaned forward, and I felt the warmth of a kiss, "That's what's next."

"What's that for?"

There was a smile in her voice, "That's because I can, and because I will again. Get used to it."

"I barfed, you know."

"Oh, I know. Next time, brush your teeth."

Della half-carried me to the helicopter while the soldier led the way. Fox and Ranger trotted along with us.

The world spun and swayed as we took off, but I managed to hold myself together. The woman kept me steady, holding me all the way through the flight. I vomited only once, and I didn't pass out at all.

Small victories.

Baby steps and small victories.

Colorado
Near Peterson Air Force Base
October 11
Year One of the Plague Recovery

The coffee is warm and black, and I take my time drinking it, enjoying every drop with a nearly hedonistic satisfaction. Even now, after a year, coffee tastes like a luxury. I hope I never take it for granted again.

I stroke my beard as I let my thoughts collect themselves and settle in comfortable corners of my brain. Yeah, I've kept the beard, and I'm keeping it short, as a wise lady recommended some time ago. I'm keeping my hair a tad long but neatly trimmed. If it weren't for the fact that I wear standard army-issue clothing, I'd almost pass for a high school English teacher.

I relax on a porch, watching the day take shape around me. More luxuries I could not have imagined a little more than a year ago.

Fox and Ranger are curled up nearby, taking in the morning warmth along with me. There's a busy day ahead, but the morning is perfect for relaxation and we're making the most of it.

The plague of the undead, what we now call the Argus/Jones Pandemic, scoured the planet unhindered for three years. I was on the road for most of that time, fighting my way through the undead and through monsters that were all too alive. In all that time, unknown to me, every remaining human effort was being spent on gathering resources and finding a way to fight back against the re-animates.

My own journey created a role for me in this fight; gave me an unlikely part to play. I would not know that for a long time, until I came to the place where I am.

I absently rub a patch of skin on my forearm, just above my wrist, a place where a dotted silver line denotes the perfect arc of a scar. I glance down at the old bite wound, now completely healed. I had spent nearly three years in the wilderness and had come out here.

I am that most rare and unexpected sort of person: a survivor of Argus/Jones.

I owe my survival to a pair of words that still have the power to strike me like a thunderclap, acquired immunity.

You see, once upon a time, I forgot my flu shot. The flu, seeing an opportunity, came and kicked my ass. Then I was hospitalized in one of the last traffic accidents of the outbreak's early days. I was pumped full of antibiotics to stave off infection, even as my body continued its production of antibodies to deal with the last of the flu. Within my body simmered a stew of microscopic defenses given support and a little extra kick from the works of twenty-first century medicine.

That medicine, coupled with my own slow recovery from the flu, would combine with an as-yet unsuspected effect of Argus/Jones. The effect? Something I had seen in my travels. It was the absence of decay among the dead. I had seen corpses weathered and mummified, but never decayed. Even the re-animates halted their decay after a certain point. That was all because Argus/Jones slowed the growth of microscopic pathogens to a crawl.

In retrospect, that made sense. The virus would need a mechanism to keep the host mobile for as long as possible. Otherwise, it would never spread beyond isolated pockets. It might even die out altogether. So, an airborne mechanism of Argus/Jones invaded every single-celled organism it could find and reduced it to a sleepwalker. Those pathogens reproduced and spread as they would in the ordinary course of nature, but their reproduction was hobbled to a snail's pace.

Fortunately, Argus/Jones couldn't spread to complex hosts in the way it spread among microbes. The virus still needed the security of a bite to successfully spread from one unfortunate host to another. That was a big break for humanity. I'm not sure we deserved it, but I'll take it and be thankful.

And what did this mean for me? The antibiotics they gave me at the hospital dealt with the pathogens that were, even then, slowing down, and that gave my immune system the chance to focus its undivided attention on the flu. My antibodies wreaked havoc on that virus and stayed in my system long after they should have, alert for the slower-growing micro-organisms.

When I was bitten, Argus/Jones confronted a weaponized immune system; one that remembered my war against influenza. It was Argus/Jones' bad luck that it shared a partial protein coat with the flu. It wasn't much of a sharing, less than a handful of receptors, but that was more than enough for me. My antibodies recognized the new virus and happily started beating the crap out of it.

When I was in the worst throes of my infection, I was already recovering. I just didn't know it at the time. If I had, I would have bundled up in a blanket and waited for the boys to come back once I'd kicked the virus to the curb. As it was, I came dangerously close to trashing all the hard work done by my immune system and those doctors long dead. If I'd succeeded in my plan to check out early, my immunity would have been buried with me.

Thank you, all gods who look after fools, that I was such a lousy shot. The bullet that I'd intended to fire into my brain had grazed my skull, instead. My confused condition and weak grip on the weapon threw off what should have been a lethal aim. I came away with nothing worse than a scalp wound and the Queen Mother of all concussions. Every morning, I comb my hair over the scar I carry as a memento.

It's interesting to observe the reactions of people here when they see me. I'm one of maybe a hundred people with an immunity to Argus/Jones, and the only person known to have earned that immunity the hard way. For the first couple of months, soldiers and civilians alike had viewed me with something near to superstition. I was the man who had come back from un-death. I had crossed that darkest ocean, sailed the River Styx, then had turned around and sailed back. I suppose I'd have felt the same way if it had been somebody else surviving Argus/Jones and if I had been the person seeing them.

Sometimes, the people here would leave little gifts of pet treats for Fox and Ranger. That's the mark of kindly people right there. They do things for those who are in no position to repay the deed. Well, if good luck is contagious, then I hope we gave those people a healthy dose of it.

Besides, the boys deserve all the pet treats they can get. If it hadn't been for them, I would never have strung those lights to celebrate that winter holiday with my buddies. And those lights, bright against a darkened landscape, would never have been seen from space, and the news would never have been radioed back to the people at Peterson Air Force Base.

Yeah, the inventor, the maker of movies and dreams and low altitude linked satellites, had made his way to the space station constructed under his guidance and with his bankroll. It wasn't an urban myth, after all. He had, indeed, ridden up on the last rocket from the Cape and had boarded that metal outpost. He was the person who saw my winter lights, and who set the stage for a search that would eventually find me.

He is still there, in his space station, and he will die there. Even if we could send a ship to him now, he has spent too much time in near-zero gravity to come home safely. He will live a long time where he is, and he seems to be happy with that. From his high perch, he minds the satellites and guides the radio traffic from point to point on Earth, and he ensures our safe communication with the moon. The human base there survives, after all, though it was touch-and-go for a while. Its people have clawed a living out of the rock in the Sea of Crises. One day, we will reach them again.

I think of what will become of the man in the space station. I know that, in the course of time, he will die, and his outpost will become an orbiting sarcophagus. Eventually, it will plunge back to Earth in a blaze worthy of any funeral pyre. Long before then, I hope he will be remembered as someone who kept us connected. I hope people will point to that moving star within the multitudes of the night sky, and I hope they will tell their children about the person who made sure that the lights never fully went out, no matter how dark it got.

Say what you will about the Hollywood of the old days, but at least it gave us one real-life adventurer who rose to the heroic.

Back here on Earth, we have begun to rebuild even as we battle the re-animates to their ultimate extinction. We are in contact with other nations, all of us struggling together to come back from the brink. Every day, the struggle takes us a little farther from the precipice and a little closer to firm and solid ground.

The air base, like many of its kind, has been in a good position to hold against a siege. It doesn't matter whether the opposition is composed of living troops or the re-animated dead, the base has been well-provisioned against just about any contingency. Power and water are being provided through a variety of sources, all of them hardened against everything that some very creative minds could imagine. Those minds had gone to work on these problems long ago.

Cheyenne Mountain didn't fare as well. One of the infected got through the mountain's security and began infecting others. Someone inside the complex set off an emergency protocol and sealed the mountain. It is closed and on a time lock. It will be years before the complex can be re-opened by any of us on the outside. It can easily be re-opened from the inside if anyone has survived, but after four years it appears nobody has. The main entry remains closed, and the mountain remains sealed.

The dog tags belonging to the fallen guardsmen now rest in a vault at the air force base, with the names and the stories of the honored dead remembered and recorded. I gave the tags to the base commander, myself. There was no formal ceremony, just a meeting in her utilitarian office. She took the tags and thanked me for delivering them. Then we sat down and split a pot of coffee, toasting absent friends.

I left the office with a feeling of real accomplishment. I had made a promise years ago, and I had kept it. Maybe there are a few ghosts resting easier because of that.

The President is helping coordinate the nation's battle and recovery efforts from the Capital in Philadelphia, and she is working with her counterparts everywhere across the globe. We have all learned a hard lesson about the cost of keeping secrets and building walls. Clinging to old animosities and the old way of doing things damn near killed every last one of us. Nobody is in the mood to repeat those mistakes.

The re-animates still outnumber the living. We estimate no more than a billion souls still live and breathe on this planet. The surviving re-animates account for another four billion or so, painting a sobering picture of the toll this plague took on all of us. The fight is not over, though the tide has turned in our favor.

We battle to thin the ranks of the undead while nature works as a steadfast ally. Vines, trees, and even mosses slowly overtake those undead who stay immobile, waiting with their unnatural patience. The green, knowing more of patience than the re-animates, consumes the undead and reasserts itself. In time, there will be nothing but forests where once the undead stood in their numbers.

Nature is changing this world in more than leaf and bough, though. The animals have begun to change. I was right about Fox, Ranger, and the rest of their kin, despite my ignorance of animal ways. The animals are growing more intelligent. No one knows exactly why or how, but it's happening. We've been getting reports from everywhere, and those reports all say the same thing. Domestic and wild creatures are behaving in ways that were virtually unknown before the plague.

Intelligence is on the rise, and a new kinship is taking shape among the living things of this world. In the wild, that means smarter predators are chasing smarter prey. Elsewhere, the partnerships between humans and others are growing deeper.

And, well, I've got a feeling that sooner or later we'll all be in for some changes in our diets. Good luck enjoying a steak when Mama Cow decides it's a good day for a stroll and you don't look too busy.

Oh, we are part of a world that is radically changing and reinventing itself, all part of our long road back from the edge of near extinction. I am at peace with this. Stasis equals death, and we've all seen where that road leads. No, thank you. I'll take this road, with all its unknowns and new horizons.

And what is my part in this? I'm just one of the people pitching in, that's all. So, call me a fellow traveler. Yeah, that fits. I like the sound of it.

I spare a quick look at the inside of my elbow and the small bruise from a needle. I grin to myself at the sight. Well, okay, maybe I've been doing a little bit more than the bare minimum. I've been donating blood, making sure my antibodies can be whipped up into a proper vaccine for everyone. So, I guess there's that. It's a little something to help us all and to make the road a little smoother.

That vaccine works pretty damn well, if I do say so. Our scouting teams and other responders were given the first jabs since they're the people most likely to encounter the re-animates. The shot makes you a bit woozy for a day or two, then you perk right up again. We've had a couple of scouts get bitten in the field, and the worst they got was a stern lecture and a tetanus booster. I can only imagine the relief that comes from knowing that a re-animate's bite is no longer an automatic death sentence.

So, we're working on it. We're working to reach the day when the undead will be a chapter in history and not a looming presence, when night will no longer be a thing that brings the chill of fear or the scent of the grave. If you are reading these words, we're working to reach you, too.

I feel a pair of arms drape themselves over my chest as a soft cheek presses against my own. Della is behind me, hugging me, and her warmth is such a gift. A smile has made its home in her voice and her eyes have learned to laugh again.

We both had hard paths to travel, though I believe hers was harder than my own. Yet somewhere along the way, the two of us learned to dismantle those walls that we all build to shield ourselves from feeling too much. We have met in a place where no barriers exist, and where walls are nothing more than ruins, relics of a dead past.

I think of my travels, of the long road that brought me to her, and I treasure feelings I never thought I would have again. My time in the wilderness taught me how to survive. Della taught me what it means to be alive. Some nights I listen to her beside me, breathing as people do when their sleep is deep and untroubled, and I feel something beyond a sense of peace. Light illuminates a place I had never known was dark.

Long or short, dear one, I will stay with you for the rest of my life.

The boys have taken quite the fancy to her, as well. Ranger loves romping outdoors with her and, more than once, I've caught Fox curled up in her lap, purring and daring me to do anything about it. Wisely, I have chosen to do nothing.

Her breath, warm and so very alive, brushes against my whiskers, "How is the journal going?"

"I'm almost done."

"Good," she kisses me on the cheek. "When you're finished, get your pack and get outside. We'll be waiting for you by the helicopter. Don't take all day, okay?"

I grin at her and return the peck on the cheek. "Yes, ma'am."

I rinse out my coffee cup and call out to Fox and Ranger.

"Okay, boys! You heard the boss. Time for us to get it in gear and get going."

This will be my final entry in this journal. It is time to write the last chapter here and to prepare for new chapters to come. Those chapters will involve you. I want you to know that, whoever you may be.

If you are alone or in a small community, barely holding your own against the re-animates and wondering if anyone is out there to help you, then hold on. We are coming. One way or another, we will reach you. Stay as strong as you can and know that there are people who can help you, who *will* help you. We are coming from rebuilt military bases and civilian strongholds, and we are actively looking for you. We will find you. Take these words as a promise.

If you are one of the vanishing ranks of warlords or slavers, holders of petty fiefs, know that we are looking for you, too. We are coming for you, and we will make no bargains. We cannot afford to tolerate the intolerable. You have the single chance of these words to change your ways. You can turn away from your paths of violence and dreams of empire, or you can face every action we can bring to bear. The decision is yours. Think very hard about it.

It's time for me to go now, time to upload this journal and time for the boys and I to get moving. There's a pair of helicopters outside and I can hear the rotors starting to turn as their engines warm up. We'll be heading to a small community of people who have been waiting for us, and hoping against hope that there was someone who had not forgotten them. We'll be on the way in a few minutes.

The boys and I pack up and I make sure to check our gear before we leave. About a half dozen troops, mostly construction and medical, are waiting for us at the helicopters. *She's* waiting for us, too. So, it's time for us to get a move on.

I hope to see you out there. I'll be looking for you, and I'll be looking forward to meeting you, whoever you may be. There's a lot we can do together.

We have a world to rebuild.

-SEND-

Afterword

There is a place in every book where an author asks you to take a minute and please read something, not just skim over it. In case you haven't guessed, this is that part for me.

The fact is, writing can be a solitary thing, but nobody ever writes alone. There is always a community backing the author. The members of that community aren't always visible, but they're always there; and you'd better believe they're always appreciated. So, I'd like to introduce you to a regrettably incomplete list of people who have helped me through this.

First of all, this book would never have seen the light of day without two singular individuals. The first is a fellow named Chris Kosarich. He is a writer of horror and science-fiction. All told, definitely a gentleman who knows how to spin a proper tale. I'm honored to call him a friend. If you get a chance to read one of his books, by all means take it.

The second person is Erin Al-Mehairi, my very patient editor. Chris introduced us. Erin, thank you for helping me navigate new and unfamiliar waters, thank you for answering all my questions ... sometimes more than once ... and thank you for your guidance and your hard work. You made this a better tale than it would have been otherwise.

I should let the rest of you know that Erin is a solid author in her own right. When she isn't editing, she's writing.

To the Lady Elizabeth, I am in your debt for your assistance as I navigated the new waters of publishing and cover art.

Next, thanks are due to the inhabitants of a place called Blackbird Comics and Community, located in Maitland, Florida. The people there go to great lengths to make this place a haven for the creative folks in the area. It truly is a community. The coffee is very good, too. When you visit, you might see me there. I'm the guy in the Harry Potter glasses, pecking away at a keyboard. Thanks to David, Candice, Eryn, Sarah, Piper, Sam, Karli, Parker, Courtney and all the rest for listening to my ideas, and for letting me park here and type all of this, day in and day out.

Needless to say, thanks go to my wife, who has run screaming from the living room on more than one occasion when I ran some story idea past her. She has a low threshold of horror so, thanks, mamasan. When you went all 'yikes' on me, I knew I was on the right track with something spooky.

Beau, Rachael, Laura, and Christie: I'm looking at you four when I send a hug and a thank-you. Beau, you were an excellent zombie. Laura, Rachael, thanks for being those two people on that "missing" poster in Miami. In the real world, we'd all never rest till we found you. Christie, you were a truly elegant associate.

Thanks, as well, to all the Zombies of Orlando. You people know how to bring life to un-death. Love to you all.

Vicarious thanks to the scenery of Orlando, which managed to be Miami, the Gulf of Mexico, parts of Alabama and Oklahoma, and even a bit of Colorado. Orlando, I always knew there was more to you than theme parks.

It goes without saying that a debt is owed to the talents of George Romero and Max Brooks, both of whom served as inspirational figures here. Gentlemen, please rest assured that a couple of properly subversive Easter Eggs are hidden in this book in your honor. Max, if I ever get the chance to meet you, I look forward to thanking you in person. George, if I ever meet you, well ... that'll be material for another book.

To the shades of Edgar Allan Poe and the other giants who permitted me to stand on their shoulders, I bow respectfully and breathe a silent thank-you.

Another debt is owed to Tom Hanks, who had nothing to do with this book, but who was inspirational, anyway. Whenever I felt the need for some sort of motivation, I went to one of his movies or one of the TV series he helmed. Tom, I can't explain how that worked, but I appreciate the fact that it did.

A final note of thanks goes to you, the reader. Thank you for giving this book a chance and for reading all the way through. Your support means more than you will ever know. I say this as someone who has heard these same words from many an author and artist. When you hear them from any of us, know they are true.

And one more thing: if you are a creative person, then please create. I want to see the landscapes you conjure, the universes you bring into being. I'll be looking for them.

We have worlds to build.

About the Author

Alan McBride is a resident of central Florida, and has been there long enough to remember when many of the subdivisions were orange groves. He has tried his hand at several professions, including serving as a science and feature reporter for a local radio network. He has also been an artistic photographer whose work has appeared in local installations. At this point in his life, he is chasing down his first love: writing.

Alan lives with his wife, Casey, in a home that is just the right size for them and their cats.